Las Animas
3/4/82

THE HOUSE
ON
PARCHMENT
STREET

Patricia A. McKillip

DRAWINGS BY CHARLES ROBINSON

Atheneum New York

1973

To my parents,
with love

THE HOUSE
ON
PARCHMENT
STREET

I

CAROL CHRISTOPHER PUFFED HER CHEEKS, SIGHED, and sat down on her suitcases in the middle of Parchment Street. The street was old and worn; it ended abruptly, running into a broad empty field in front of her. On one side of the street was a graveyard. On the other side was a high stone wall with a closed gate. Old trees arched over the wall; their leaves whispered softly against the stones. The long windblown grass in the graveyard played the iron railing like a harp.

The warm summer wind swooped unexpectedly across the field, opened the gate, and set it creaking aimlessly a moment. A massive square house sat firm and ancient beyond the wall, stone-grey beneath a beard of ivy. Carol caught a glimpse of it before the gate slammed shut again. The street was empty, the field was empty, and the only sound on Parchment

Street was the wind, agile as a cat, leaping over the old stone wall.

Carol stood up to get at the back pocket of her jeans and pulled out a letter. She sat down and smoothed it flat on her knee, her eyes flickering over it until she found the part she wanted: ". . . *There is no ordinary street address; the House is well known in Middleton, being something of a historical monument. There are no other houses on the street anyway, except for Emily Raison's house, which is cheerful and modest and on the graveyard side. . . .*" She looked up. A small white house with a sharply pointed roof faced the graveyard, half-hidden in apple trees. Her head turned slowly toward the closed gate and the grey house hidden behind it. She sighed again, softly, and folded the letter.

Six boys floated out of the graveyard on their bicycles. They skidded to a halt at the sight of her, colliding gently with each other. For a moment they were quiet with surprise. She stared back at them, motionless on her suitcases. And then, as though someone had pulled a string that set them in order, they flowed into a neat circle around her, spokes winking under the sun.

"Coo, look at that hair."

"Carrots."

"No, it's more like fire. I wonder what she combs it with. Should think a rake."

"Look at those dirty jeans."

"And bare feet. I wonder if she's an orphan. I say, are you an orphan?"

Carol stood up slowly. Her hands clenched, the letter crumpled between her fingers. Faces spun around her, curious, distant, mocking.

"She must be an orphan—she's nothing but skin and bones."

"She can't talk, either."

"Of course she can't. You won't let her get a word in. Shut up, the lot of you, and let her talk."

The street was silent again but for the ceaseless click-click of bicycle wheels. Carol's mouth clamped tight. She bent and picked up her suitcases.

"She doesn't want to talk."

She took a step forward. The circle melted forward with her. Somebody snickered.

"Matchstick. That's what she is: a walking matchstick, lit."

Carol took a firmer grip on her suitcases. She swung them in front of her, and in three long quick steps broke the circle, leaving one bicycle wobbling perilously. Another, jolted by a suitcase, smacked against the curb and fell.

"Ouch!"

She whirled, her face flaming. "Well, it's your own fault! I am not an orphan, and I'm sick of being told I'm skinny, and I hope your spokes are bent, and as soon as I can write a note to my aunt, I'm going home, and I'm not ever coming back to this country! Ever!"

5

There was a little silence. "Coo. She's American."

The boy beneath the bicycle pulled himself free and sat up, rubbing an elbow. He was big, fair-haired, with a slow even voice that bore no malice.

"Are you Bruce's cousin from California? Wait—" His hand went out as she turned. "What's your name?"

She stepped across his bicycle wheel and kicked the gate open with her foot. She heard his voice, slightly plaintive, before she kicked it closed again.

"He told me her name—I've forgotten—"

There was a fishpond in front of the house. Great orange fish nibbling on the leaves of golden water lilies made startled dives at her approach. The house, solid and square, had two rows of long windows and two dormer windows jutting out from its high roof. Two great chimneys rose cold, motionless against the sky. The stone wall stretched far toward the field, then angled to encompass a vast sweep of side yard.

Carol set her suitcases on the porch and pounded on the door. She waited a moment, flicking her long hair out of her eyes, and she noticed then how quietly the stones rose upward before her, and how the thin curtains breathed in and out of soundless rooms. She shifted impatiently on the steps, the anger quivering in her. She lifted her fists to pound again.

There was a muffled voice shouting from the other side. "Why can't you go round to the back? I can't—open—"

6

The door creaked again, moving a fraction of an inch. The voice belonged to a boy. Carol set her shoulder against the door and shoved.

It sprang open in a chorus of noises: a wild garbled cry; the deep curly sound of a loosened spring; the rapid beat of a clock bell counting hours. Carol caught her balance, clinging to the doorknob. For a second, she did not move. Then she peered around the door in time to see her dark-haired cousin disentangling himself from a grandfather clock.

"Of all the stupid things to do—Will you shut up?" He pounded on the grandfather clock. It whirred to a silence; the sound hummed a moment, golden, dying in the air. Bruce was silent, blinking in the dim hall. He reached up, massaging his shoulder. "What are you doing here?"

"Don't worry. I'm not staying long."

"Are you Carol?" His eyes, narrowed a little against the light, moved slowly over her. He dropped his hand, leaving behind a shadow of grease on his shirt. He moved, looking behind her. "Where's my parents?"

"How should I know?"

His eyes came back to her. "What are you angry about? It's me who should be angry, having people push me into clocks when I have to get my bicycle fixed."

"I didn't mean to push you into a clock. I don't see why you have a front door if you don't want people coming through it."

7

"Every house has a front door. I can't help it if this one is three hundred years old and has trouble opening. I'd rather live in a modern house with a doorbell anyway." He stopped abruptly. His mouth pulled downward at the corners, then twitched tight. "What —How did you get here? Mum and Dad went to pick you up at the airport in London."

Carol was silent. She swallowed suddenly and sat down again on a suitcase. "Oh, no." Her hands rose slowly, covering her mouth.

"Didn't your mother tell you?"

"I think so, but . . . there were so many people, and it was so much fun being by myself, doing things for myself . . . I just forgot. I took a bus to the station in London and then I took a train to Wellingborough and then a bus to here. Then I asked where Parchment Street was and I walked here, only I thought I was lost because I couldn't remember that there were supposed to be graves. And then. . . ." Color washed into her face; her hands closed beneath her chin into fists.

"And then what?"

She stood up. "And then I decided to go back home. I have a round-trip ticket and I'm going. At home they don't tease me. Much."

Bruce's mouth opened slightly. It curved, after a moment, into a soft, noiseless "Oh. . . ." He drew a breath. "They just aren't used to people who are— different. This is a little town."

8

"Do they do that to everybody who looks different?"

He nodded, his eyes steady, aloof on her face. "Mm. And most of the time, I'm there to help. Only I wasn't, today, because I've been fixing a flat."

In the silence, the clock started ticking again, after a soft inner click, as though some piece had fallen into place. Carol picked up her suitcases. "Well." Her voice shook on the word; she paused to steady it. "Tell Aunt Catherine I'm sorry she had to go to London for nothing."

"It's just what Dad would call facts. About me. He's a historian. After all, we don't have to like each other. You came over for a month to get cultured. To see how people in a different country live. You might as well stay for that, now you're here. You would just upset everyone if you went back home."

"Everybody here has upset me."

"People naturally upset each other. Perhaps in California, people all go barefoot with their hair in their faces, but not in Middleton. People don't—people don't like strange things." He bent down, reaching for her suitcases, and for a moment she could not see his face. Her voice came unfamiliar, distinct and needle-sharp.

"You surprised me, too. I thought you would at least be nice."

His face, pink and white in the summer sunlight, flushed to the color of an even sunburn. For a moment his eyes lost their aloofness, flicked uncertainly to her

9

face. Then his dark brows melted together into a scowl. He took the suitcases from her and turned to the staircase. "I used to be," he said. "Your bedroom is upstairs. I'll show you, and then I have to fix my bicycle. You can look around by yourself." The stairs, red-carpeted, creaked under their feet. "That's my room, round the corner. Yours is on the main landing." They turned a corner and went up a few more steps. He nudged a door open with his foot. "Bathroom's next door."

The room was small and sunlit, with a dark ancient wardrobe twice as big as the bed. There was a full-length mirror in the door of it; she saw herself suddenly in it, tall as Bruce, her hair vivid, tangled from the wind, her worn jeans doubled-patched at the knees. She turned away and went to look out the window.

It faced Parchment Street. Across the rows of grave-stones half-hidden in the trees, she saw a great grey church, its spire drifting in the moving clouds. As she opened the window, bells played a familiar four-tone melody, then tolled the hour.

"Four o'clock. Does it bother you, living across the street from a graveyard?"

He did not answer. She turned and found him standing behind her, his hands in his pockets, staring down at the graves with narrowed eyes. The color had come into his face again.

"I hate it," he said softly. "Dad likes it. He likes old things. I do, too, when they're—when they're beautiful. Like the church. But I hate this house."

He turned abruptly, restlessly. Then he turned back, leaning out the window, and shouted back at a chorus of staccato shouts and whistles that broke the mellow silence on Parchment Street.

"Hoy! I'm coming! I'm coming!"

A chain of bicycle riders poured through the gate, began to rotate around the fishpond. Carol stepped back from the window. Bruce jerked himself back in. Somewhere below a phone rang.

"That'll be Mum and Dad, I expect. Phone's in the kitchen." He vanished. She stood a moment, listening to the pound of his feet on the stairs, to the slam of the back door. She went down slowly, following the sound of the phone down the dim hall, into a big cheerful kitchen.

A woman's voice said before she could speak, "Bruce? I tried to call earlier, but you weren't there. Is Carol there? We can't find her anywhere; we think she might have gotten mislaid between here and California. Your father is checking on that, and I'm trying to think how to tell Anne that her daughter is somewhere on earth but we're not sure where—"

The smile began somewhere inside Carol before it touched her face. "Hello, Aunt Catherine," she said.

She opened the door for them two hours later, and Aunt Catherine hugged her. Then she held Carol at arm's length to look at her, and Carol, who was taller than her mother, only came up to Aunt Catherine's eyes.

"Look at that, Harold," Aunt Catherine said. "She's got my hair. Her mother's is black as a stovepipe. And such lovely green eyes. I wonder where those came from. Have you eaten yet? We stopped for fish and chips. This is your Uncle Harold."

Carol turned. A tall man with Bruce's dark hair, and smiling eyes, took the pipe out of his mouth and held out his hand.

"How do you do. Where is Bruce? Have you met him yet?"

Carol nodded. "Yes." She cleared her throat. "I pushed him in the clock."

Uncle Harold's face smoothed. He looked down at her quizzically, the pipe smoke curling upward from his fingers. "He wasn't rude to you, I hope."

"Oh—It wasn't because of that. He couldn't get the door open and I pushed. And he fell in the clock and it started banging and it wouldn't stop. But it's all right now, I think."

"Well," Aunt Catherine said briskly. "I'm sure that clock has survived worse than Bruce climbing in and out of it. Where is he?"

Carol's hand crept upward to the top of her head. "Bike riding, I think. . . . I'm sorry that you had to go to London for nothing. My mother told me you were picking me up, but I forgot. Some days—some days are like that. I forget to do what I'm supposed to, and I push people into clocks instead. I can't get coordinated. I usually end up breaking something. So now you know what you're getting for a month."

They were silent a moment. Uncle Harold said gravely, "I should think it required a definite amount of coordination to travel halfway across the world by yourself, and still manage to catch the proper train out of London. What do you think of the house?"

"Bruce said it's three hundred years old. I thought it would be more like a castle."

"It's as cold as one," Aunt Catherine said.

"Houses," Uncle Harold said, "are generally built with some degree of practicality. This used to be a vicarage, a place where the parish priests lived, and they had neither the need nor the money for a castle. Parts of it have been rebuilt from time to time, but other parts, like this stone floor and the great broad beam above the fireplace, suggest that the house was not built three hundred years ago, but rather rebuilt from an even older foundation."

Carol looked down at her feet. The worn grey stone swept unbroken toward the kitchen. She curled her toes. "No wonder it's so cold."

Uncle Harold smiled. "There. I didn't mean to begin a lecture on architecture." He turned to Aunt Catherine. "Where's the chips?"

"Here," Aunt Catherine said, "under my elbow." She shifted a roll of newspaper that smelled of hot fish into one hand, and dropped the other hand lightly on

13

Carol's shoulder. "Come and eat, and tell me how the American side of my family is doing."

They ate fish and chips out of warm greasy newspapers on the kitchen table as they talked. When Aunt Catherine finished asking about the relatives she had not seen in fifteen years, Uncle Harold poured himself a cup of tea and settled back for a discussion of American politics and education. Carol interrupted him before he got too far.

"What kind of stove is that?"

"It's a trial," Aunt Catherine said. Uncle Harold blinked, as though his thoughts were reordering themselves. Aunt Catherine stood up and lifted the two large smooth domes that covered the burners. "It's Mrs. Brewster's stove. Mrs. Brewster is the woman we rent the house from. She probably has a nice gas stove. This one runs on coal, and it has two speeds: hot and very hot. Which reminds me—I should put Bruce's dinner in to warm." She got the newspapers full of Bruce's fish and chips and opened one of the heavy oven doors. Uncle Harold looked at his watch.

"He should have been home an hour ago."

"I know."

"I wonder sometimes if he doesn't think he is living in a hotel. Is basic courtesy too much to ask of a boy his age, or is communication totally impossible?"

"Perhaps he forgot," Aunt Catherine said gently. "Why don't you show Carol the house while I do the breakfast dishes."

Uncle Harold looked at Carol. "Would you like that?" he asked, and she nodded, smiling. Then they heard the click of bicycle wheels and the slam of the porch door.

"Bruce!" Uncle Harold shouted.

He opened the kitchen door and stuck his head in. "I've got to wash up—I'm all over grease."

"Come here, please."

Bruce's hand dropped from the doorknob. He came in slowly. His eyes moved once to Carol's face in a stranger's impersonal glance. Then they dropped. "Yes, sir?"

Uncle Harold sighed. "Your mother is not a hired cook. She cooks because she loves us, and it would pain her to see us starve. I've had to tell you that too many times before."

Bruce's shoulders twitched. "Yes, sir. I'm sorry I'm late. Is that all?"

"No. Look at me."

Bruce's eyes rose slowly. They looked at each other, their eyes alike, dark and aloof. Uncle Harold said, "Mrs. Brewster disturbed me this morning with a phone call. She said she thought I should know that you spent yesterday evening sitting in a tree in the square smoking. I am not sure whether she was concerned with your health or the possibility that you and your friends might have set the town square on fire."

Bruce's mouth dropped slightly. "Was that her with the flashlight? We couldn't think who it was. She

15

didn't say anything. She usually does."

"I imagine she does," Uncle Harold said. "I don't enjoy being bothered with phone calls like that before I am properly awake, and I wish you would refrain from troubling Mrs. Brewster. I am not going to lecture you on smoking, because you are old enough to make your own decision about that. But what has been troubling me is something different. I saw a ring of boys on bicycles tormenting Mrs. Simmons' boy on his way to his cello lesson, and I was disturbed to realize that they formed a perfect, orderly circle as they rode, as though they had practiced it many times before. I was never so ashamed of you in my life."

He was quiet. Aunt Catherine's hands had stilled among the dishes. Bruce stared down at the table. Then his head lifted abruptly, his eyes going to Carol's face.

She sat startled a moment by what she read in them, and then her face blazed. "I didn't tell," she snapped. "I can fight for myself."

Uncle Harold looked at them bewilderedly a moment. Then his hand hit the table with a little smack.

"Not Carol, too—"

"He wasn't with them."

"It doesn't matter that I wasn't," Bruce said. "I probably would have done it, if I didn't know who you were."

"That's a marvelous welcome to give to guests in your own country," Aunt Catherine said tartly. "It's a wonder she didn't turn around and go home."

"She wanted to."

"I was going to."

"Well, what stopped you?"

"Bruce!"

"I'm not being rude, I'm being curious. I would have gone."

"Well, I don't like running away from things. Or people."

Uncle Harold said distinctly, "Will you please apologize to her."

"I'm sorry," Bruce said tightly. He looked at Uncle Harold. "If you see that circle again, there won't be me in it. Ever."

He turned and left. Uncle Harold dropped his head into one hand. Aunt Catherine washed dishes with a harsh, rhythmic clatter. Then she slowed and turned to Carol, sitting mute in her chair with her hair hiding her face. Aunt Catherine wiped her hands on her apron. She sat down beside Carol.

"I'm glad you didn't go," she said softly.

Carol's shoulders moved in a little shrug. "I'm used to being teased. I'm skinny, and I'm taller than half the boys in my class, and my hair looks like a haystack on fire, and I can't walk up to the blackboard at school without stepping on somebody's lunch. But most of the time, I don't let people bother me. I can't fight all of them."

"Well, you're wiser than I was at your age. I

17

couldn't go down the aisle either without tripping over my big bony feet."

Uncle Harold dropped his hand. "Your feet aren't big and bony." His voice was tired.

"They were then," Aunt Catherine said. "I don't know what's troubling Bruce these days. He rarely talks to us, and we can't read his mind. The only thing I can do is leave his fish and chips in the oven for him and remember that once he had a very sweet smile."

Uncle Harold's mouth relaxed. He looked at Carol. "Well," he said gently, "are you still in the mood for a guided tour?"

Carol sighed. "Yes. If I wake up hungry in the middle of the night, I don't want to get lost."

There were four large rooms on the ground floor: the kitchen; a room across from it that Uncle Harold said had been the morning room where the vicars had once eaten their breakfast, but which was now Aunt Catherine's laundry room; the living room connected to the kitchen, with a great, fat-legged round table, and a fireplace built of huge squares of grey stone and dark, heavy, smoke-blackened beams; and the room across from it, Uncle Harold's study, with his desk and papers and endless shelves of books. Upstairs were four bedrooms.

"It's a bit big for us," Uncle Harold said, "but I like old things. Most of the furniture belongs to Mrs. Brewster. She was born in the house. Her father bought it when the church across the way turned Catholic again after four hundred years, and the new priests decided they didn't want to support a large, rather chilly historical monument. Mrs. Brewster lived here until her husband died, and then she began to rent the house. I've had my eye on this house for several years, but it wasn't until last winter that we were able to rent it from her."

"Why did the church turn Catholic? I didn't know churches did that."

"The old Protestant parishioners died or moved away until there weren't enough people to support the church. Sometimes, when that happens, the church is destroyed to make room for something else. But the Catholic population in the town had grown out of its own little modern church, so they bought this one instead of building a new one. It was Catholic, of course, when it was built first, because it is nearly eight hundred years old."

Carol drew a slow breath. They were climbing the last part of the stairway, that led to the rooms beneath the roof. "My father gave me a silver dollar once that was made in 1887. That was old, to me."

Uncle Harold smiled. "You live in a young country." They reached the landing. There were two small rooms, one on each side of the hall. "This is where the maid and the cook would sleep, if we had them. Now they're Mrs. Brewster's storage rooms."

Carol went into one. She knelt down on the window-seat between the thick walls, and looked out. Uncle

Harold unlatched the window and opened it. The scent of cool grass mingled with his sweet pipe smoke. A single star hung beyond the high dark tower of the church.

"It's so quiet. . . ."

"Mm."

"At home, there's a freeway running near our house. I can hear trucks on it even late at night." She looked down. "I wonder how Emily Raison can stand living in a graveyard."

"It doesn't seem to bother her. She doesn't like dogs, or cows in fields when she goes blackberry picking, but she's not afraid of graves. There's no reason to be. The people in them lived in the same world you and I live in, and often their thoughts about it were not very different from ours. Well. You've seen everything except the cellar and the gardener's shed and—"

Carol turned. "There's a cellar? I've never been in one."

"Good heavens. Come along, then. I should go down anyway and get coal to feed the stove tonight."

"Do you leave it on all night?"

"Oh, yes. It would take hours to heat it up properly every morning." He switched on the hall light as they went downstairs, and said meditatively, "I can't decide which Catherine hates most: the stove or the stone floor in the hall. It is dreadfully cold during winter."

He stopped in the kitchen to get the coal bucket, then led her to a little door behind the main staircase.

She smelled cold stones and damp earth as he opened it. He switched on the light, and she saw narrow, worn stone steps leading to a great black mountain of coal at the bottom. She followed him down and looked around as he cracked coal bricks with the edge of the can. There were two rooms beyond the coal room; in the first one she found a freezer and a water tank and a cat licking itself on a pile of rags.

Its eyes caught light from the coal room and blazed at her like cut amber. Then they vanished as the cat turned and slipped silently into the third room. Carol followed it.

"I didn't know you had a cat." She crouched at the doorway and called it softly.

"We don't."

"There's one down here."

"Is there? They slip in, sometimes, through the broken windows. Emily Raison's cat Geraldine had a litter of six down here once. Is it calico?"

"No. It's black. It's male." She called it again, her voice high, coaxing, and it moved across a table of old china and fragile figurines so smoothly it seemed only a shadow. It faded imperceptibly into the shadows, and she blinked, suddenly finding nothing to call. She moved into the room, looking behind stacks of boxes of books, old picture frames, more china. The grey cellar stones in the twilight were thick and old as the stones of the outer wall of the house. She saw a movement out of the corner of her eye, and turned toward the window. She saw beneath it the slow fading of a man walking into the wall.

The touch of Uncle Harold's hand on her shoulder jolted her. She shivered.

"I called you," he said gently. "You didn't hear me."

She looked up at him. His face was calm, familiar behind his pipe. The full coal bucket was in his hand.

"You're frightened. What's the matter?"

Her mouth was too dry for speaking. She swallowed. And then she laughed, drawing a little jerky breath. "It was your shadow, going across the wall. It scared me. I thought—it looked like—it looked like somebody walking into the wall."

"I'm sorry. I didn't mean to frighten you. Don't let the house trouble you. It creaks quite a bit, but I doubt if there are ghosts wandering through the walls."

He followed her back up, switching the lights off behind him. She turned suddenly at the top of the stairs and looked down into the dark rooms. Uncle Harold waited patiently. Her brows crept together. She looked at him puzzledly.

"But I wonder where that cat went."

II

IN THE LIVING ROOM THEY FOUND AUNT CATHERINE knitting in a rocking chair beside the fireplace. The fireplace, built of red brick with a mantel of dark rich paneling, was enclosed in a deep alcove of thick stone from which unfamiliar things hung, gleaming in the lamplight. Aunt Catherine's mouth was set in a straight grim line. Carol looked over her shoulder to see what she was knitting, and she dropped her hands in her lap with a sigh.

"What is it going to be?"

"Heaven knows. I want it to be a scarf. Emily Raison is teaching me. She can knit whole sweaters."

"It looks all right," Carol said. She sat down on the brick ledge in front of the fireplace. Uncle Harold came back from putting coal in the stove and sat down, dusting his hands. Something clanged faintly in back of him, and he shifted his chair forward. A brass frying pan with a four-foot handle swung gently against the stones behind him. Carol leaned forward to look at it.

"What is that?" She raised the hinged lid. "It's too heavy to be a popcorn popper."

Uncle Harold laughed. "It's an antique bed-warmer. The vicars didn't have electric heaters to warm their rooms, so they put coals in the pan and warmed their sheets before they went to bed."

"There are times when I've been tempted to use it myself," Aunt Catherine said, frowning at her knitting.

"You can't say you weren't warned," Uncle Harold said. "I warned you about English weather, but you married me anyway."

"I was young and innocent. I wonder why there is a hole in the middle of my scarf. . . ."

Carol looked behind her at the row of fragile tea-cups on the mantel. She shifted, leaning back against the stones, and glanced up to find a dark, unfamiliar shape hanging over her head. She stood up and reached for it.

"Be careful," Uncle Harold murmured. "It's heavy."

The weight of the iron ball pulled her hand downward. She caught at it and numbed her fingers against the spikes protruding from the ball. She shook her hand absently, staring puzzledly at the arrangement of the ball, linked by heavy chain to a polished wooden handle. Then she said,

"Oh."

"It's a flail. Knights used them during the Crusades. I expect they were quite effective."

"I bet they were." She weighed it experimentally in her hand. The dark ball swung back and forth like a pendulum. "I can't imagine really killing someone with one of these. There wouldn't be much left of him, and you would have to see it. . . . It's a little like a baseball bat, I guess. You adjust the weight over your shoulder and—"

The door opened, and Bruce came in. He stopped abruptly as Carol turned, and the iron ball, swinging gracefully through the air, smashed one china cup to splinters on the mantel and knocked another to the floor.

The ball bounced painfully against Carol's elbow, but she did not seem to notice it. She stared horrified at the bits of cup at her feet. Uncle Harold took the flail from her limp hands and hung it back up.

"It's a bit damaging to civilization," he commented. Bruce closed his mouth. He held out a letter.

"I came—I just came down to give you this. The postman gave it to me this morning so he wouldn't have to bother climbing the hill." His voice shook and he stopped. Carol raised her head. Her eyes glittered with tears.

"I'm so sorry—" she whispered.

"Never you mind," Uncle Harold said. Aunt Catherine leaned over the side of her chair, a suspicious pucker at the sides of her mouth.

"Soon as I finish this row I'll sweep it up. Don't cry. Mrs. Brewster has dozens of bone-china cups."

Carol sniffed. Her face, half-hidden from them in the fall of her hair, had flushed red. A tear trickled down to the edge of her chin. Aunt Catherine dropped her scarf. She put an arm around Carol and led her to the kitchen.

"She'll never miss them."

"It's one of those days when everything goes wrong—"

"I suspect you need a hot bath and a good sleep."

"I don't think that's going to help." She wiped her face on a dishtowel while Aunt Catherine took a bottle of milk out of the refrigerator. "I don't know if this house will be able to stand me for a month."

"It's stood all kinds of people for more than three centuries," Aunt Catherine said. She shook the milk bottle and poured half of it into a pan. "The first thing I broke in this house was a hideous Victorian vase shaped like a green Chinese dragon. Harold accused me of doing it deliberately, and I think he may have been right." She smiled as Carol laughed in the middle of a sniff. "Why don't you go up and get ready for bed, and I'll make you some hot chocolate to take to bed with you."

Half an hour later Carol sat in bed drinking chocolate and listening to the house creak around her as it settled in the night air. Through the open curtains she

27

could see patterns of stars above the swaying graveyard trees. She reached down once and tucked the covers more securely around her feet. The wind, still through the long twilight, had risen again, fresh and chill. The church bells tolled a quarter hour half-muffled by it. Carol finished her chocolate and lay back. The events of the long day ran in a kaleidoscopic stream through her mind. She rolled over, drawing the covers in a hood over her head and shifting her feet to find a warm spot between the cold sheets. The wind whispered through the eves, shook the window, then turned and sighed away through the trees. A floorboard cracked somewhere in the house. Carol rolled over again. She sat up finally and drew her knees under her chin and rubbed her feet. They were icy. She sat for a moment, holding them. Then she reached for her robe and went quietly downstairs, sliding down the banister.

She took the bed-warmer and the hearth shovel from the fireplace and brought them into the kitchen. She found the coals in the stove behind a small door on the side. The thick heat pushed against her face as she shoveled coals into the bed-warmer. She added a few more to the stove from the half-empty coal bucket, closed the door, and replaced the shovel. Then she found thick dishtowels in a kitchen drawer and wrapped them around the pan. The warmth melted through them to her hands as she carried it down the cold hall, up the stairs. She put the pan between the bed sheets and lay down, resting her feet on top of it. She drifted to sleep lulled by the night wind and the soft pulse of heat slowly thawing her feet.

Aunt Catherine's cry jerked her upright in the morning almost before she could open her eyes. She heard doors opening and rolled out of bed, kicking the bed-warmer open. A stream of ash fluttered to the rug. She struggled into her robe and ran into the hall, nearly bumping into Uncle Harold, who was leaning over the banister with a razor in his hand. There was a trickle of blood in the lather on his face.

"Catherine," he said. Bruce's door opened. He came out tying his robe, his hair sticking up.

"What's the row?"

"No coffee," Aunt Catherine said succinctly. "No breakfast. Harold, I will never cook another thing on that stove. You can gift-wrap it and leave it on Mrs. Brewster's front porch."

"Catherine, what happened?"

"I don't know! I know I closed the coal door last night; I remember distinctly checking, but it wasn't latched properly, and it may well have burned the house down."

Uncle Harold went downstairs, wiping the soap off his face. Bruce followed him, not noticing Carol on the landing above him, standing white and still, her cold hands covering her mouth. She heard their voices from the kitchen and moved finally.

The heat welled from the open kitchen door, warm-

ing the hall floor. The stove, both round burners un-
covered and red hot, seemed to shimmer. Aunt Catherine stood looking grimly at it. Uncle Harold opened
both oven doors.

"I don't understand it," he said.

"I do. Impulse."

"Catherine, not even this stove acts on impulse—"

"Aunt Catherine," Carol said. Her voice sounded
small, dreamlike in her ears. They turned to her, as
though hearing an unexpected note in it, and she drew
a long breath. "It was me."

"You," Aunt Catherine said blankly. Carol gave a
little nod.

"Yes. I needed coals. For—for the bed-warmer."
Their faces were still around her, bewildered. Her voice
dwindled. "My feet were cold."

Uncle Harold stared at her. He gave a sudden odd
moan. Then he sat down at the table and laughed until tears ran down his face, and Aunt Catherine's face
twitched into a smile in spite of herself. Carol watched
them, too numb to laugh or cry. She looked up and
found Bruce's eyes on her, the aloofness in them over-
come by incredulity. She looked away. Uncle Harold
straightened finally, and wiped his eyes on his sleeve.

"Do you always do things the hard way, Carol?"

"I didn't think," she whispered. "All I could think
about was my feet."

"Well, after all," Aunt Catherine said. "That's what
bed-warmers are for. Carol, if you don't latch that small

30

door tightly, the coals will overheat from too much air. That's why we always check it at night. So I can have coffee in the morning without melting the bottom of the pot."

"I'm sorry."

"I'll find you another blanket tonight."

She nodded. Then she sat down, tucking her cold fingers under her arms to warm them. She heard the soft sigh of Bruce's breath.

"We're biking to Wellingborough today, Dad," he said. His voice was dazed. "I'll be home for dinner." Uncle Harold stared after him in amazement as he went out the door. Aunt Catherine shook her head.

"Shock," she said, and Carol smiled. She leaned against the table, her head in her hands, and the color came back into her face.

"I was so scared to come down here my feet got cold all over again. I've done a lot of things, but I've never nearly burned a house down."

"Never mind," Aunt Catherine said. "The stove should cool down by suppertime. I'll go and brew some tea on Emily's stove. Did the bed-warmer work?"

She nodded. "But I knocked it out of bed this morning, and there's ash all over the place."

"You slept with it?" Uncle Harold said.

"I thought—that's what they're for—I wrapped it in towels—"

Uncle Harold's hand went to his robe as though he were feeling for his pipe. He didn't find it. "It's unorthodox. And a bit dangerous. . . . Catherine, I need a very, very strong cup of tea."

"I need another stove," Aunt Catherine said.

Carol wandered outside after breakfast. She climbed an apple tree in the back garden and sat in it awhile, looking far out over the green fields that dissolved into a mist at the horizon. The church bells tolled ten o'clock, clear in the windless morning. She jumped down, threaded her way carefully between neat bean rows, and went toward the front gate. She looked out; the road was empty. She crossed it and found a path on the other side that ran in front of Emily Raison's house into the graveyard.

The great grey church stood at the end of the path. On each side of it were rows of high rounded stones, tilted and sunken with age. Long grass grew up their faces, covering worn letters. A cat napped, balancing delicately on one of the stones, its paws tucked under its breast. Beneath it, a little round woman in high boots knelt washing the face of the stone.

Carol leaned against the railing, watching. The cat, splashed with color like a patchwork quilt, yawned and settled itself. It opened both eyes at the sudden movement by the railing as Carol hoisted herself up. She landed on her knees on a grave, and the cat made a startled leap off the stone. The old woman straightened as Carol rose, dusting her jeans.

"Bless me." She sat back on her heels, looking a little

uneasy. Then she smiled, and her face wrinkled like a sun-dried apple. "Hello, my dear. You must be Catherine's niece."

Carol squatted down beside her. "How did you know?"

"Oh, she showed me a picture of you and said you were coming. You look different from the picture, else I would have recognized you straight away."

"That was my mother. She made me look nice. What are you doing?"

"I'm washing gravestones. This one belongs to my cousin Harriet. If I didn't wash them, they'd get all dirty and mossy. I cut the grass round them too, else they'd be overgrown with weeds. That one over there is my uncle's—that one with the beautiful fat cherub."

"Are you Emily Raison? Why do you live in a graveyard?"

Emily Raison dipped her cloth in her bucket and cleaned the dirt out of Harriet's name. "I was a maid in Mrs. Brewster's house when I was a young girl. I went to this church all my life, and this is where I belong. So I saved my money, and when I had enough, I rented the little house from Mrs. Brewster. Do you like the big house, then?"

Carol looked down the path to the high wall and the rise of the big house behind it. She touched her hair. "I think so. I'm not used to things being so old. . . . I don't know how to treat old things. And the house is so quiet, and it creaks."

"It was a great noisy thing in Mrs. Brewster's day when she was a young girl, and her father had people in and out. I was always busy."

Carol rested her chin in her hands. "I wish I was," she said. The cat returned unexpectedly to rub its face against her knee. Emily Raison rinsed her cloth and wrung it out.

"I expect you're homesick."

Carol looked at her. "I expect I am," she said, surprised. Emily Raison heaved herself to her feet.

"You come with me, my dear, and we'll have a nice cup of tea. Come along, Geraldine. That's Geraldine, my cat. Don't they look nicer, now? So much brighter, because they have someone to look after them."

"Don't the other ones?"

"Most of them are too old. Hundreds of years old."

She picked up the bucket and led Carol to her gate. Someone passed them: a young, fair-haired priest in a black cassock who called as he went by,

"Good morning, Miss Emily. Have you been washing your relatives?"

"Good morning, Father Malory. Yes. Don't they look lovely?"

"Bright spots in a wilderness. Hello, there."

"Hello," Carol said, and he whisked past like a cheerful, energetic crow to be swallowed up in the shadow of the church.

They had tea and raisin buns in Miss Emily's neat kitchen. Miss Emily talked in her gentle, cheerful voice

34

about her life long ago in the big house, about her myriad relatives, living and dead, and about how hard it was to climb the sloping hill up to the churchyard after she went shopping. The bells rang unheeded quarter hours as she talked, and Carol's eyes glazed, and she began shredding a raisin bun into her cold tea. The bells struck twelve, and she woke a little to count.

"But Susan wouldn't stay," Miss Emily was saying, "no matter how Mrs. Brewster cried. She was always a passionate little girl, Mrs. Brewster was, and she loved Susan. But Susan wouldn't stay, not after what happened in the cellar."

"What happened in the cellar?" Carol asked mechanically.

"Oh, my dear, she never told anybody."

"Oh."

"She was just a little bit of a thing, not much older than you, and so fearful about breaking things when she dusted. And when she ran up shrieking with her apron over her face we couldn't think what she had broken in the cellar when there was nothing but coal. And she had hysterics, right in the library in front of two visiting priests. She never would say what happened."

"Never?"

"Not a word. She was so delicate I thought she wouldn't last long, but two years later I got a nice wedding picture from her, and she lived to have five children."

Carol swallowed a yawn. "I should go," she said. "Aunt Catherine will be wondering what kind of trouble I'm in now."

Miss Emily accompanied her to the door. "Well, you tell your Aunt Catherine she can make whatever she likes on my stove while hers cools."

Carol blushed. "I will. Thank you—thank you for cheering me up."

Miss Emily patted her hand. "You come anytime you like, dear."

"Goodbye."

Miss Emily closed the door. Carol threaded her way through the maze of the colorful garden. Then she stopped. On the other side of the gate, blocking it with his bicycle, was a familiar, fair-haired boy.

Carol's mouth pinched into a thin set line. She glanced back at Miss Emily's door, but it was firmly shut. So she walked to the corner of the yard, stepping delicately in the pansy bed, and climbed onto Miss Emily's white fence. The boy coasted in front of her before she could jump down.

"You're still angry," he said. "I can tell." He put out a hand to balance himself. His eyes were grey and undisturbed.

"Will you please move."

"Please, I want to talk."

"I know. If you had known I was Bruce's cousin, you wouldn't have called me a matchstick." The color flared into her face at the word.

36

"I wasn't going to give you an excuse. We were rotten, that's all. You aren't a matchstick, Carol. That's your name. I remember now. I'm Alexander."

"I want to get off Miss Emily's fence."

Alexander sighed. "Oh. Right, then. You're still angry, and you won't talk. . . ." He rode slowly beside

her as she walked, her chin high. "Will you just answer a question? Just to be polite. Where's Bruce?"

"He went to Wellingborough."

"Mm. He had intentions to go, then. . . . He does that, sometimes, you know. He sort of vanishes. Without a word of warning. Everyone else went to Wellingborough. But then, what's in Wellingborough? I mean, why should he go there, if he doesn't choose to?"

Carol looked at him. "He didn't go there?"

"No. So I thought I'd look round for him a bit, because I'd rather go nowhere with Bruce than somewhere with everyone else. You know."

Carol opened the gate. "I don't know why you would," she said crossly. "I wouldn't like to go as far as the other side of the street with him." She closed the gate and went across the lawn toward the front door, standing open to the still summer day. She heard her name called before she reached it. She saw Alexander's face between the leaves above the high wall.

"I'm really quite nice inside," he said, smiling helpfully. "I say, if you see Bruce, tell him—"

The sharp slam of the door cut his sentence short.

She saw Bruce finally in the late afternoon as she sat on the window-seat in her bedroom chewing the end of a pen, with an unwritten postcard on her lap. He came slowly through the gate, wheeling his bicycle. He walked stiffly, his head bowed, and bits of his clothing fluttered oddly. She straightened slowly, seeing even from that distance the long weals on his forearms.

Aunt Catherine came out of the laundry room as he wheeled the bike to the porch. He let it down easily, kneeling beside it. He looked up at them as they came out the back door, and his face was a map of angry scratches.

Aunt Catherine knelt on the walk beside him. "Bruce, what happened?" She turned his face gently from his bicycle so she could see it. He sighed through stiff lips.

"Two flats. And the body is so scratched."

"I noticed. Bruce, what happened to you? You look like you tangled with an irate zoo."

He was silent a moment. His eyes flicked to Carol's face, then away. He sighed again, his hands moving over a torn tire. "Oh . . . I wasn't thinking. . . . They saw a picture at Wellingborough this afternoon. I met them when they were coming home. . . . They took a shortcut through the fields where Emily Raison does her berry picking." He paused again. The wheel spun futilely under his hands. "Well. They were all excited about the picture. It had a man in it—Steve McQueen. And he had a motorcycle, and he could jump anything with it—hills, hedges, walls—anything, as long as he had the momentum. All he—all he had to do was jerk the front wheel up and sail over—"

Aunt Catherine touched her eyes with her fingers. "I see. Oh, Bruce. Don't tell me—"

"Well, you asked me to. And it seemed a good idea at the time. We did have a hill for momentum, but I can't remember why we chose a blackberry hedge to jump over."

Something broke inside of Carol. She sat down on the sidewalk and gurgled helplessly into her knees. "Steve McQueen on a bicycle," she gasped. "I can just see it. Even if you had cleared the blackberries, you would have bent the bicycle frame landing—"

She felt the sudden coolness of Bruce's shadow as he stood up. She lifted her head. "How do you know? I suppose you've done that, too. No. Perhaps you had sense enough not to do *that* at least—"

"Bruce!"

"I didn't laugh at you when you broke Mrs. Brewster's teacups swinging the flail, or nearly burned the house down to warm your feet. They were good ideas, even though they didn't turn out, and it's not fair of you to laugh at mine."

Carol rose. Her eyes glinted. "I didn't know you wanted me to be nice to you."

"I don't! I'm talking about fairness—"

"So am I, and you couldn't be fair about anything —especially niceness—even if you wanted to be, which you don't!"

Aunt Catherine looked up at them helplessly. "Shall I make you a scorecard?" she suggested. Bruce's fists clenched. He stepped across the bicycle and went into the house. The slam of the door rattled the porch windows.

Carol folded herself into an angular shape on the

walk, her knees bent, her head hidden in her arms. "I'm sorry," she said after a moment. Her voice was muffled. Aunt Catherine spun the bicycle wheel. Light danced endlessly from one spoke to another.

"I'm not," she said reflectively.

Carol went to curl up again on her window-seat. She rested her chin on her knees and stared outside and saw nothing. The house was quiet around her, as though it were drowsing in the afternoon. Light fell in a change-less pool on her floor boards. She stirred restlessly, hunched against herself, and saw the fishpond, open water lilies burnished in the sunlight. The trees were motionless beyond it. She hugged her knees in a tighter grip, and loosed her breath in a slow weary sigh. Then she uncurled, her feet hitting the floor with a thump. She went aimlessly downstairs, sliding down the banis-ter when the stairs began to crack sharply. She sat a moment on the end of the banister, her chin in her hand, staring at nothing. The living room door opened so abruptly she jumped.

"Harold! Oh, Carol. I'm glad you're still here. Fa-ther Malory is coming to dinner tonight, and I haven't been able to use the stove, besides forgetting I even asked him—Would you mind going down to the cellar and getting a blackberry pie out of the freezer? Thank you, dear. Harold!" She touched the top of her neat hair lightly in despair. Carol dismounted. She heard Uncle Harold's shout back, as she opened the cellar door and over it, Aunt Catherine's voice calling upstairs. "Bruce! I need some flowers!"

She found the freezer in the room beyond the coal cellar and shifted things in it until she found a pale pie in a plastic bag, neatly labeled. A shadow leaped onto the freezer lid as she closed it, and she jumped, then laughed. The great black cat slipped through her hands so sleekly she barely felt it. She followed it into the last room where it scratched its claws a moment on Mrs. Brewster's table, then began threading a private maze on the floor, through boxes, stacks of mildewed books, dusty figurines, until it leaped up on the table and then into the window-ledge, brushing as it leaped the dark crown of the broad-brimmed hat of a man.

He stood still as though he were listening for a sound in the quiet house. Beyond the thick stones church bells tolled four o'clock, distant, leisurely, as from another world. His face was a still cold silhouette beneath the flow of sunlight from the cracked window. He turned abruptly, a drawn sword in his hand, and walked into the wall.

III

CAROL LEANED AGAINST THE CELLAR DOOR, HER HEART leaping against her ribs, her mouth dry as if she had been running. She reached behind her and pushed the bolt that locked the door. Then she eased down to the floor and rested her face against her knees, the pie bag in one limp hand at her side. Her heartbeat slowed gradually; she began to hear sounds about her: the rattle of pans in the kitchen, the back door closing, footsteps in the hall. They stopped in front of her. She jumped, but instead of a strange, dark, somber face, she saw only Bruce's face, patterned with scratches. He held a handful of daisies. She swallowed the dryness away from her throat. He was quiet a moment. Then he drew a breath, as though to speak. Uncle Harold came out of the study, and Bruce closed his mouth.

"What in heaven's name," Uncle Harold said, "did

43

that to your face?"

"A blackberry bush. I rode into it."

"It looks very painful. Did you put something on it?"

"No. I—No."

"There must be something in the house. . . ." He turned Bruce slowly, surveying the damage, and Bruce's shoulder jerked under his fingers. "It looks like you dove into it headfirst."

"I think I did."

"Come upstairs; we'll find something." He looked down at Carol, sitting on the floor. "What's the matter? You look like you've seen a ghost."

She swallowed, but her voice came in a whisper. "I think I have."

"Oh. In the cellar?"

"Yes."

Uncle Harold shook his head. "Remind me to investigate that shadow of yours. Bruce—"

He followed Uncle Harold stiffly, the daisies trailing on the stairs. Carol sat a moment longer, staring at the chill grey flagstone. She got up finally and took the pie into the kitchen.

"Aunt Catherine—"

"Four, five, six," Aunt Catherine said, counting potatoes. "Thank you, Carol—just put it on top of the stove so it can thaw. Now, will you look in the cupboard by the door and get out the lace tablecloth and spread it on the round table in the living room. Where

44

is Bruce? I didn't ask for a whole floral wreath."

"Uncle Harold is putting something on his scratches." She found the tablecloth and carried it to the living room. She unfolded it and flicked it open so it floated through the air and settled lightly on the table. She leaned on it, staring down at the delicate endless pattern. "Aunt Catherine," she said softly, "I saw a man in your cellar with a black hat like a Pilgrim on his head and a sword in his hand, and he walked into the wall as though it wasn't there. . . ." Her voice sounded small, unconvincing in the quiet room. The sun picked out the deep tones of mahogany beneath the lace. She rubbed her eyes again with her fingers, and her shoulders slumped. "Aunt Catherine, I want to go home. . . ."

"Heavens," Aunt Catherine said behind her, "this room is a wreck." She straightened the pillows on the couch and picked up sections of the morning newspaper off the rug. Bruce came in, still carrying the daisies. His face was streaked with white. Aunt Catherine glanced at him.

"What is that all over your face?"

He shrugged irritably. "I don't know. It came out of a tube."

"You look like a zebra."

His mouth twitched into an unwilling smile. "I do, rather. I can't find a vase for these, and I've looked everywhere."

"There's a blue one in the kitchen."

"Oh, Mum, I can't put them in that. It's too small. There's a symmetry involved . . . I know. There's one in Dad's study." He went out again. Carol watched him cross the hall. She took a strand of hair and wound it around her chin. Then she straightened.

"Aunt Catherine—"

There was a hissing sound from the kitchen. "Excuse me, dear," Aunt Catherine said hurriedly. "I think my potatoes are boiling over."

Carol sighed. She twitched the tablecloth straight. Bruce came back in with a green vase and she said, "What's symmetry?"

His eyes slid to her face, surprised. He put the flowers on the table and started pulling away the leaves. He said after a moment, "It's when things balance. When they match one another in proportion. Like this house. The outside is symmetrical—the windows on one side are in the same position as the other, and the door is exactly in the middle. Some houses, old ones especially, might have one big window on one side of the door, and a little one on the other. Like the house is winking one eye. That's not symmetrical." He began putting the flowers into the vase. She watched them build under his hands into a white pyramid. Aunt Catherine came back in with plates and silverware in her hands. She pushed the tablecloth aside and set them down.

"That's lovely, Bruce. Thank you. Now, will you go outside and shake the leaves off the tablecloth. And then go change your shirt."

He murmured absently, tugging gently at the pyramid. He gathered the cloth in his arms and went to the front door. Carol followed him slowly.

"Bruce," she said, as he tugged open the door. His head turned, his eyes meeting hers almost uncertainly. He whipped the cloth open, scattering leaves on the steps and on the head and shoulders of Father Malory, standing silent with surprise on the doorstep.

Carol gave a startled hiccup of laughter and stilled it with one hand over her mouth. Bruce's face flushed crimson. Father Malory brushed the leaves off his sleeves as though he were used to doing it.

"Hello, Bruce. I thought that might be your cousin, when I saw her this morning. Catherine said she had red hair. How do you do? I am Father Malory."

He held out his hand, a leaf dangling from the black cuff. Carol shook hands with him. Bruce ran a hand through his hair.

"This is Carol Christopher. I'm sorry about the leaves. I didn't see you in time."

"I'm thankful it's only leaves. Do you know, two or three centuries ago, people weren't so careful about what they threw out of their windows and doors without looking. Good afternoon, Harold. It might as easily have been the remains of yesterday's stew." He shook hands with Uncle Harold. "How is your article on Viking activity in Scotland coming?"

"Fairly well," Uncle Harold said. "It will probably involve another trip North before I have to begin

47

teaching again, but I don't think Catherine will mind that. Come in. I'll show you part of it." He opened the study door. "Sit down. Would you like some wine?"

"I would, thank you."

Uncle Harold paused a moment before he went out. "Have you been gardening?"

"No. I have no talent for that. People don't even trust me to water the flowers in the church. Why?"

"You have an unusual amount of leaves in your hair."

"Oh." Father Malory brushed at them. Bruce went back into the living room and spread the tablecloth out again. Carol picked a stray leaf off it.

"He's nice. I didn't know priests were nice."

"What did you think they were like?"

"I don't know. Gloomy. They wear black and talk about what happens after you're dead."

"People's clothes don't matter."

"Yes, they do. You try going into a little town with bare feet and patched jeans and then say they don't matter."

He set the flowers precisely into the center of the circle. "That's different. Priests have always worn black. It's traditional. That's why you can't tell what a priest is like from his clothes. But if a priest wore jeans and went barefoot, then his clothes would matter to other people. Why don't you wear dresses and comb your hair?"

"I do comb it!"

"Well, it never looks combed. I'm not trying to start an argument; I'm just saying that you look the way you do most likely because you don't want to look the way somebody that you don't like looks."

"Or because the people I like dress this way."

"Well, then, you aren't going to like anybody in this town." He went to the door. He paused before he opened it. "What were you going to say before I dumped the leaves on Father Malory?"

"Never mind," Carol said crossly. "I think you like starting arguments. You don't like people liking you. And I do like people in this town. I like Emily Raison, and your parents, and Father Malory. And I think I like Alexander."

"Alexander?"

"At least he smiles." She went into the kitchen. Aunt Catherine, mashing potatoes, looked up at the abrupt closing of the door. Carol sat down at the table and ruffled her hair with her hands angrily.

"I'm going to throw my comb and brush away. Then he'll really suffer."

He was quiet during dinner, keeping his eyes on his plate while Father Malory and Uncle Harold discussed the church across the street through half the dinner until they were interrupted.

"I know the bell-tower was destroyed in a fire thirty years ago, which accounts for the different color of the stones, but I don't believe the late Gothic style was altered any in the reconstruction," Father Malory was

49

saying, and then the sudden shrill of whistling just beyond the windows broke his train of thought. He looked toward it interestedly. "I never realized before how much a group of boys whistling sounds like Irish banshees wailing for the souls of the dead."

"I didn't either," Uncle Harold said. "Bruce, why don't you go out and tell them you're eating before they shatter all Mrs. Brewster's antique glassware. Bruce."

He blinked, and looked away from Father Malory. "What?"

"Please go and tell your friends you are having dinner," Uncle Harold said patiently. Bruce left. There was a little silence. Carol swallowed a mouthful of chicken and cleared her throat.

"Uncle Harold?"

"Yes, Carol."

"Did—did Miss Emily ever tell you about Susan?"

"Susan? Not that I recall. Why?"

"Oh, I remember Susan," Father Malory said suddenly. He wiped his mouth with his napkin and laid the napkin down in the butter. "Susan the maid, who had a dreadful experience in the cellar and hysterics in the study?"

"Heavens," Uncle Harold said. "I missed a good one."

"Yes," Carol said. She swallowed, as though she had a word stuck like a fish-bone in her throat. "And I was wondering. I was wondering if she saw a ghost. In the cellar. At home—I've seen movies about old English castles and houses, and they have ghosts in them. So maybe Susan saw a ghost."

"There are no such things as ghosts," Uncle Harold said firmly. "Whatever happened to Susan in the cellar was either caused by another person or her own imagination. And whatever you have seen in the cellar is probably the natural result of being for the first time in your life in a very old house that happens to stand across the street from a graveyard."

"I've always wanted to see a ghost," Father Malory remarked placidly. "But nothing exciting ever happens to me, not even when I go through the graveyard for midnight services."

Carol shivered. "I wouldn't do that for any reason."

The door opened. Bruce came back in and sat down quietly. He shifted the butter dish from underneath Father Malory's napkin and set it aside. Aunt Catherine said thoughtfully:

"I wouldn't be surprised if there were a ghost down there. We have everything else—mice, spiders, batches of stray kittens. It's probably the ghost of some poor vicar who got burned in his bed using a bed-warmer."

"A ghost down where?" Bruce said abruptly.

"Nowhere," said Uncle Harold.

"Did Carol see something in the cellar?"

"Susan did," said Father Malory.

"Susan who?"

"Susan the maid, about fifty years ago," Uncle Harold said patiently. "She had a frightening experience, Miss Emily said, and Carol was wondering if it were possibly a ghost, owing to the reputation that old English houses have in America."

"Oh." He drew breath softly. "Oh."

"Why," Father Malory said curiously, "would a vicar want to sleep with a bed-warmer?"

Uncle Harold laughed. He felt in his pocket for his pipe. "Why don't we have coffee in the study, and with Carol's permission, I will tell you a little story about bed-warmers."

Aunt Catherine gave Carol a tray of coffee to take to them while she cleared the table. She heard their voices, calm and unhurried, as they talked of the great stone church, and the late sunlight warmed the old stone beneath her feet. She put the tray on a table between them, and looked around as Uncle Harold poured coffee. Light traced the gold titles of books standing row upon row almost to the ceiling, or stacked sideways on the desk, on the floor. It fell in a pool on the cold grate in the fireplace, touched the rare tones of gold in the painting above the fireplace: the picture of a girl standing in a dark arch of stones, her face sober, intent as though she were listening for some sound beyond the canvas. Her long dress was deep blue; the white lace on her cuffs and the square collar showed delicate and rich against the darkness.

"Who is that girl?"

"Nobody knows," Uncle Harold said. "Not even

Mrs. Brewster. No one knows who painted the picture, either. Do you like it?"

"Yes. Those stones. . . . She looks like she's standing beside the house or by the wall."

"Mm. It's strange. A mystery painting. It's nicely done."

"Mrs. Brewster had someone in to date it once," Father Malory said. "I believe he decided it had been done in the last century. It's odd, isn't it."

Uncle Harold was silent a moment. "Yes. She looks like she might have lived in the house when it was first built."

The blue eyes of the girl gazed down at them, quiet, preoccupied, and they were quiet again, looking up at her. Then Father Malory said apologetically, "I seem to be dripping on your rug. . . . Oh, I see. I have managed to dunk my sleeve in my coffee. I wonder sometimes if I am fit company for civilized men."

Carol climbed one of the tall trees that grew over the front wall the next morning, and sat hugging the trunk swaying like a ship's mast in the strong wind. She stared out at the neat rows of grey headstones, looking as weathered and immovable as old trees. The wind lulled her; she closed her eyes to the flickering sunlight and let her thoughts glide silently through her head until she was half-asleep among the rustling leaves. The noon bells roused her finally; she counted and then the thought came to her and her eyes flew open. She

54

moved her face from the branch and felt it stiff, patterned with bark. She stared at the quiet gravestones.

"Twelve," she whispered. "Midnight. He's a vampire, and he lives in the cellar. . . ."

She leaned over, and gripped the branch she was standing on, and swung down. She landed on the grass and got up, dusting her hands.

"Hello," said a disembodied voice.

She whirled, her heart pounding. Alexander smiled at her.

"It's only me. Flesh and bones and teeth. I came to see Bruce, but he has faded away again. So I was meditating by the fishpool when suddenly this great wild beast sprang out of a tree at me. But it's only you."

"I didn't see you come down the street."

"Well, I didn't see you hanging in the tree." He paused a moment, one eyebrow tugging upward thoughtfully. "I wonder where he goes when he goes."

Carol brushed the grass off her knees. She moved toward the house. "I don't know. Why don't you ask him?"

"I do. He gives me vague mumbles." He walked beside her, his hands in his pockets, his step long and easy through the grass. "Perhaps he goes off to grow hair all over him and howl at the moon."

"I wish you wouldn't talk about things like that."

He glanced down at her. "Is it the graveyard? Does that make you nervous? People in it are dead. I don't see why people should do things after they're dead that

55

they wouldn't do while they were living. Though perhaps that's no comfort."

Carol stopped suddenly on the porch. She drew a breath to speak, and held it a moment while one foot traced the letters in the welcome mat. She said finally, "Do you believe in ghosts?"

"No. Not outside of people's minds."

"Oh." Her mouth crooked. She nudged the door open with one shoulder. Alexander moved forward to lounge in the doorway before she closed it.

"Why? Do you think you've seen one?"

"Yes. It had big green teeth and spider webs in its hair, and I'm probably going nuts."

"Crackers," Alexander said. "Over here you go crackers. Words are funny. Do you want to come for a ride on my bicycle and help me look for Bruce?"

"No."

"Oh." He removed himself from the doorway with a sigh. "Right. If you see him, tell him I was here."

But she did not see him until long after dinner, until Aunt Catherine and Uncle Harold sat sipping tea in the living room while the sky beyond the church steeple turned blue-grey with the late summer twilight. Carol sat curled on the window-seat, watching the twilight outline the tree leaves and freeze them into a motionless pattern. Something danced once past the window, too big to be a moth, flickering too much to be a bird.

"A bat," said Uncle Harold. She jerked back. Then

she saw Bruce slip like a shadow through the gate.

The back door closed softly a moment later. Uncle Harold put his cup down. He rubbed his eyes with his fingers. The stairs began to creak.

"Bruce!"

The creaking stopped. It descended slowly. The living room door opened. Bruce stood mute in the doorway, his mouth set while they stared at the rainbow-colored bruise on one eye that clashed awesomely with the scarlet scratches.

"What happened now?" Uncle Harold said feebly.

"I fell off my bike."

"Oh, Bruce. Your bicycle is in two pieces on the back porch."

His hands rose suddenly in an angry desperate gesture. They were shadowed grey. The blunt ends of pencils stuck out of his pockets. "Can't you leave me alone? All right—I was fighting. But that's my affair! I have to work it out for myself!"

In the silence came the soft futile tap of moths against the bright window. Uncle Harold said softly, "I'm sorry. I won't meddle."

Bruce's mouth opened, then closed. His head dropped; his hand moved back and forth across the door knob. "I'm sorry I'm late. I didn't want to come home." He closed the door as he left.

Uncle Harold looked down at his teacup. He picked it up and held it without drinking. He put it down abruptly; it clattered in the saucer.

"I never know how much to say!"

"I know," Aunt Catherine said gently. The corners of her mouth were tight. "It's hard to know." She put her knitting aside and rose. "I'll make a cold-pack for his eye."

Uncle Harold picked up his cup and followed her into the kitchen. Carol heard the murmur of their voices behind the closed door. She leaned her head against the windowpane, feeling the glass cold against her face. She rose finally and went into the hall.

A sheet of paper lay on the grey stones. She picked it up. It was coarse drawing paper. On the other side of it was a picture of the church. She stared at it, moving slowly up the stairs. The church rose brilliant against the rising sun, its shadow swept back to uncover hunched worn gravestones. In the dim hall light she could see the delicate stonework ornamenting the lean arched windows, the patterning of glass in one great window that opened like a rose to the sunlight. And in one corner of the graveyard, curving with a tuft of grass, she found Bruce's name.

She swallowed, something inside of her fluttering with excitement and fear. She went up the stairs to the closed door at the end of them. She knocked softly. She heard the sudden roll of bedsprings and the creak of floorboards. The door opened to Bruce's face, twisted painfully into a scowl. It melted a little into surprise. She held out the drawing.

"You must have dropped it when you came in."

He looked down at it without moving. Then his face moved, and he reached out for it. He held it, his breath still, the color rising slowly in his lowered face.

"I didn't know," Carol whispered. "I never knew before that when you see a beautiful drawing, there's a person who has done it."

His face rose. The unbruised eye looked at her, uncertain, unguarded. He said hesitantly, "I got up, before the sun rose. I climbed on the roof, so the trees weren't in the way."

"Is that how you got your black eye? Falling off the roof or something?"

His brows pulled together. He looked away from her. "No. I was sitting in a field drawing a cow." He opened the door, and his eyes came back to her face. "I think —There's something else I'd like to show you. Come in."

He went to his window-seat. It opened like a chest, and he reached into it for a tablet. He sat down on the floor, leafing through it. Carol watched the pictures flicker between his fingers.

"How long have you been drawing?"

"Three years."

"And nobody knows? Doesn't Uncle Harold know?"

His hands paused. "No."

"But he likes pictures."

"He likes facts. I just want to do things my own way, without being bothered or—or teased by anyone." His mouth tightened suddenly. He looked down at the tablet, turning drawings without looking at them. Carol watched him for a moment, her brows crinkled. She drew a silent breath, and said tentatively, "Is that—is that what happened? They teased you?"

His eyes rose surprisedly. "How did you know?"

"If you had got kicked by a cow, you would have said so."

"Mm. I wish I'd thought of it." He leaned back against the window-seat and said wearily, "They came —they came so suddenly I didn't even have time to hide things. And they did what—what we always do to people—what we did to you. There was a picture of flowers—that's when I tried to stop them, when they teased me about that one. I was so angry I couldn't see. I don't know who I was fighting with—I didn't care. I never want to see any of them again. I didn't want to see anyone. So I drew until it was too dark to see, and I had to come home." He caught his breath in a slow sigh and turned pages slowly in the notebook. "It's hard to get a proper perspective with only one eye working. . . . Here it is. This one, I drew a few months ago, just after we moved in." He held it out to her. Something brushed feather-light down her back as she looked at it. Her mouth opened, closed again, wordless. Her voice came finally, small, tight.

"Then I'm not nuts."

IV

Out of the taut vivid mask of Bruce's face, his good eye gazed at her, wide and steady. "You did see him then. You did see him. I thought you had, but I wasn't sure, and I was—I didn't want to ask you straight out if you'd seen a ghost in the cellar walking through walls—did you see him walk through the wall?"

"Yes."

"I thought I was going barmy. I tried to tell Dad, but Dad would have—he believes in facts. Things happen for a reason; things can be proven. I didn't tell him. But one day—one day I brought him down with me to see it—he nearly walked right through it. I was scared. I've been scared in this house ever since we moved in last winter, but Dad loves it. So I'm never home much."

Carol hugged her knees. She rested her head on them a moment. "What—what's he doing down there? Is he a vampire?"

"A vampire?"

"They wear black. They live in cellars."

"Oh." He picked up the picture and studied it. "I never thought of that. . . . I don't think so. Vampires don't exist, anyway."

"Oh. Just ghosts."

"Well, he hasn't bitten anybody, has he? Look." She raised her head. "Look at his clothes. I've never seen a vampire dressed like that."

"He's got a black cloak on."

"I know, but it only goes to his knees. And he has a white collar and white cuffs. And that hat like a cowboy hat with a high crown. And he doesn't act like he sees us, but. . . . More like he's waiting, looking for somebody from his own time."

"When was his own time?"

"I don't know."

"I don't understand," Carol said bewilderedly. "What's he doing down there? Why is he walking through walls? People don't walk through walls when they're living—why should they do it when they're dead? Why does he haunt a cellar waiting for somebody who won't come?"

"I don't know. Unless—"

"Unless what?"

"Unless . . . unless the other person does come.

Perhaps there is more than one ghost."

She shifted. "One is all I want to worry about."

"I know, but—What's the first thing you did when you saw him?"

"I ran."

"So did I. But suppose someone else came while we were running. Or something else happened, that might explain what he's doing there."

"I suppose you want to go down there and wait for him. Maybe he's not doing anything but walking through walls. Maybe he likes walking through walls."

"Why should he walk through a wall? People walk through doors in walls because there's a place to go to on the other side of the door. There's nothing on the other side of the wall but dirt and earthworms."

"I knew it. I knew he was a vampire. He probably has a coffin in the graveyard."

"Rot. In a church graveyard? Vampires don't like churches. They don't like crosses. I think we should go down and wait for him and see if he does anything we didn't see before that might explain him."

Carol eyed him reflectively. "All right. But if he starts growing fangs, I am going to run, and I'm not going to stop until I get to California. I think you should warn people about things like that before you invite them."

He smiled. He said after a moment, "I didn't invite you. But I'm glad you're here. Now I can stop being frightened and start being curious."

63

There was a knock on the door. He closed the drawing tablet and put it back into the window-seat, letting the top down soundlessly. Carol got up off the floor. Bruce opened the door. Aunt Catherine, a damp towel full of ice in one hand, looked at them, startled. Bruce flushed slightly.

"We were discussing vampires."

A corner of her set mouth twitched. "I knew you must have something in common. Bruce, lie down and put this on your face for a few minutes. Your dinner is in the warming oven." Her voice firmed as he opened his mouth. "I know you don't want anyone to do anything for you, but this is for my sake: I don't like having to look at your face in that condition, and I don't want to have to worry about your eating habits."

Bruce sighed. "I was only going to say thank you. I haven't eaten anything all day."

They waited, the next afternoon, an hour among Mrs. Brewster's dusty china and damp books, in the stillness of the old cellar. Sunlight strained through the streaked broken glass into a pool that widened across the table, spilled over onto the floor. The bells measured the passing moments, drew them into quarter hours, and at the third quarter their soft talking slowed. Bruce glanced at his watch, reset it. Carol shifted on the table, overturned a teacup, and righted it.

"Four o'clock. That's when I saw the ghost."

He nodded. "I've seen it three times, and each time

64

I heard the bells. I wonder . . . do you suppose that's what he was listening for? The bells? I wonder what happened at four o'clock that day he waited in the cellar when he was alive."

"Whatever it was, he didn't go through the wall when he was alive."

"No."

"Oh. I forgot to tell you. Alexander was looking for you yesterday. He—"

"I don't care what he was doing," Bruce said abruptly. His face turned away from her toward the window. "I don't want to think about them."

She was silent, running one finger around the teacup rim. "He wasn't there, was he?"

"Yes."

Her hand stilled. It dropped, limp, back into her lap. Her head bowed until the fall of her hair hid the light falling across their faces. "Oh. . . ."

They were silent. Someone walked in front of the house; a shadow dropped across the window, vanished. Floorboards creaked from Uncle Harold's study above their heads. Carol swung her heel against the table leg, her mouth pulling downward.

"I thought he was nice. . . ." The sudden touch on her arm stopped her. The bells rang four o'clock across the peaceful summer day. In front of the grey wall a man stood listening, waiting.

Bruce's breath gathered and stopped. The face was pale and thin-lipped, the dark hair cut blunt just below

the ears. The watchful eyes touched their faces a brief moment, and Carol froze. Then the eyes passed indifferently away, and the man turned and walked into the wall.

Bruce's voice shook a little near Carol's ear. "Did you see the sunlight on his sword? How could it flash like that off something that wasn't real?"

"I don't know. Why are we whispering?"

"I don't know." His hand closed suddenly in a painful grip on her arm. "Carol—"

A girl walked out of the fall of sunlight toward the wall. Her long dress brushed the boxes of Mrs. Brewster's books; they heard the soft rustle of it. Her hair fell in butter-colored curls to her shoulders. The white

cloth of her square collar and cuffs was spotless in the light, and the lace that edged it was delicate and rich.

She turned and looked at them; one hand touched the old stones. Her eyes were deep blue. She said softly, "Edward. Come." And then she turned and faded through the wall.

A sound like a whimper came from Carol's throat. She swallowed, and it came again. Bruce turned and looked at her. His face had gone white; his eyes were wide, dark, speculative.

"The girl in the painting. . . . Don't cry."

A tear trickled down the side of her nose. She brushed it away. "I'm not. I was—I can't—I don't understand any of it. Who is going to come next?"

"I don't know." He stared at the stones as though they were not there and he could see what lay beyond them. Carol watched the serene fall of sunlight uneasily. A shadow melted through it, and she jumped. Bruce's head turned sharply. The amber-eyed cat leaped up beside him and picked a path through the figurines. He leaped up to the window and squeezed through the broken pane.

The bells rang the quarter-hour. Sun slipped behind a cloud, and the light faded from the stones, leaving them old and worn. Bruce slipped off the table. "Come on."

Carol nodded. She followed him up the stairs slowly, out the front door, across the side lawn where the warm grass, newly mowed, smelled sweet, crushed beneath their feet. Bruce stopped beneath a grey cherry tree beside the wall. He swung himself up and came to rest in the crook of a strong branch, overlooking the broad field and the flat world beyond. Carol found a comfortable spot below him. She leaned her head back against the broad smooth trunk.

"I'm so tired."

"Mm. That's from being nervous all afternoon." The tree trembled faintly as he shifted. "I feel like I'm trying to work a jigsaw puzzle with half the pieces missing. Who is Edward? Why was she telling him to come through a stone wall?"

"She wasn't telling Edward to come. She was talking to us. She looked straight at us."

68

"How do you know she saw us? How could we follow her through a wall?"

"In the painting it wasn't a wall."

Bruce was still. He swung off his branch and landed on hers with an abruptness that made her cling to the shaking tree. "It was an arch," he breathed. "You're right. An arch of stones. . . ."

"In the cellar?"

"I don't know. I don't know." He pounded softly, rhythmically on the branch, his eyes narrowed on the far fields. He said slowly, "I've got an idea."

"What kind?" Carol said suspiciously. He picked a leaf and tore it delicately along the veins.

"Just a hunch." He tossed the leaf-bits away and looked at her. "A hunch about ghosts, and graveyards at midnight. . . ."

"No."

"Think a little. If there's two ghosts walking round in our cellar as though they still live there, what do you think happens at midnight when ghosts are properly, traditionally supposed to come out? If we can see ghosts when nobody else can, we can see them wherever they are, at any time. Aren't you curious to see if there's any truth in that?"

"If we can see ghosts, we can also see vampires, werewolves, witches, and Frankenstein's monster."

"Frankenstein's monster was only in a book. Carol, that sunlight—it wasn't right. They had shadows. They weren't real, but they had shadows. Whose sunlight were we sitting in? Ours—or theirs? Who was real, then? Us or them? Were they in our time? Or were we in theirs? Or is time something like the house, where stones from different centuries exist side by side, and where people from different centuries can talk to each other?"

"I don't know. It sounds scary. I still don't see why we have to go sit in a graveyard at midnight."

"I want to see if they come out at midnight. Perhaps the girl was buried in the graveyard. She probably was, if she lived in this house, because people didn't move around so much before cars were invented. And perhaps we can find her tombstone, find out when she lived, what her name is."

Carol grimaced. "Why should she come out at midnight? It's cold and wet and dark."

He sighed patiently. "Ghosts do. It's traditional."

"It's also traditional for witches and werewolves to exist. Suppose we do sit out there, and everyone comes out—there's bound to be a vampire around somewhere, and it's traditional they bite you in the neck, and people find you the next day stiff as a board without a drop of blood in your veins. What would my mother say? What would your mother say?"

"At this point, I don't think my mother would be too surprised at what happens to me. I'll go alone, if you're frightened. Shall I? But in the cellar, I didn't think you were afraid of anything."

Carol eyed him coldly. His voice was guileless, but

the corners of his mouth curved. He grinned suddenly, the scratches pulled awry across his face, and she laughed in spite of herself.

"Oh, all right. But if anything horrible happens, I will never speak to you again."

"No, I don't expect you will," he said reflectively.

She sat at her window watching the moon hung like an eye above the church steeple when Bruce tapped at the door. She opened it softly. He said, "You'll want shoes."

"Why? It's my neck they'll bite."

"I know, but there will be slugs all over the grass."

She put on her shoes without a word. They crept through the hall by the light of Bruce's flashlight and slid down the banister. The house was soundless in the quiet midnight. They went out the back door. The night smelled richly of damp earth and cut grass. Moonlight glanced silver off the corners of the house.

"The moon is full."

"Sh."

The gate creaked faintly as they opened it. The long grass blades curved silver against the cold iron of the graveyard fence. The spire loomed above them, a shadow against the stars, and moonlight brushed the ancient arches of the windows. Carol brushed close to Bruce, her hands tucked under her arms. The faint chill of their breaths drifted mistlike before them.

"Emily Raison's house is so dark. . . ."

"She's in bed."

"Most people are in bed. Sensible people, who don't believe in ghosts, who wouldn't dream of coming out at midnight to sit on a gravestone and—What's that?" Her fingers closed on his arm.

"Emily Raison's cat," he said patiently.

"What's she doing out at midnight?"

"I don't know. Cats keep odd hours. Come on." He swept the light toward the side path. "Let's go over the fence here. There's a tree we can sit in." He pulled himself up. The sharp railing points glittered like spears. He was still a moment, balanced between them. She heard the soft whisper of his sigh. "It's different, thinking about a graveyard and being in one. It looks so quiet. . . ."

"Just wait." She swung a leg over the railing.

"It seems like there should be rain and thunder. . . ." He slipped down and focussed the light. The worn stones stood waist-high, tilted, shadowed from the clear moon by hunched, aged trees. Carol jumped down beside him, and the midnight bell began to toll.

Bruce was still beside her; she saw the flicker of his eyes across the ancient graves. He touched her, and she jumped.

"Sh—" His voice was the tendril of a whisper in the hushed air.

"I want to get off this grave. Suppose somebody wants out?"

He looked down. Grass moved under the light,

72

springing straight where he had first stepped. He moved slowly at first, almost jerkily. She stared after him. The last bell pealed, echoing into unendurable silence.

"Come on—"

His head was a dark patch above a gravestone. She moved finally, crouched beside him. From the deep fields came the dreaming cry of an owl. Footsteps, faint and steady, came toward them down the path.

Carol's hand pressed against her mouth. Bruce's fingers curled warningly about her wrist. His breath rose and stilled. The footsteps grew louder; a shadow slipped soundlessly from stone to stone. Something flashed starlike from the moving figure. Bruce's hand tightened. Carol hid her face abruptly in her bent knees.

"I'm going to be sick."

"Sh—"

The footsteps stopped. Bruce shifted; his flashlight scraped against the stone. There was an odd whimper from the ghost. Bruce breathed a short incoherent word and rose.

An explosion of light drenched him. A neat elderly woman in a coat and hat pointed a formidable flashlight at them. The terrier at her heels set up a frenzy of barking.

"Bruce Lawrence! Does your father know you're out?"

"No, Mrs. Brewster," Bruce said wearily. "But I expect he will."

73

"I don't understand," Uncle Harold said at breakfast the next morning. "What were you doing in the graveyard last night?"

Bruce pushed a cold crumpet around his plate with one finger. Sunlight fell in a cheerful pool on the table; from the stove came the crackle of eggs slowly frying. Aunt Catherine turned away from them to listen.

"Was it Mrs. Brewster on the phone?" she asked, and Uncle Harold nodded.

"She was out walking her dog, and she saw a light flickering in and out of the gravestones. Being naturally fearless, she investigated, and found my son, who as I recall, said he was going to bed at ten o'clock last night." He shook his head. "I don't mind if you run about in graveyards in the middle of a summer night as long as you don't damage property. But if you feel you absolutely must do such things, I wish you would refrain from annoying Mrs. Brewster."

"What were you doing there?" Aunt Catherine asked. Bruce tore his crumpet slowly in half. He sighed.

"I'm not really sure, now. It seemed—it seemed like a good idea at the time. We thought—I mean I thought—"

"We thought," Carol said. Uncle Harold's eyebrows rose.

"You, too?"

"I did the thinking," Bruce said. "I don't think I did very well."

"But what were you doing?" Uncle Harold said be-

74

wilderedly. Carol's eyes flicked to Bruce's face. It was lowered; his mouth was set in a taut, stubborn line. He lifted his head suddenly.

"Dad—"

"We were looking for ghosts," Carol said. Bruce glanced at her, startled. Aunt Catherine's eggs began to smoke behind her, but she did not notice them.

"Ghosts?"

"They come out at midnight."

Uncle Harold eased back in his chair. He took a sip of tea. "Did they?"

"No. Mrs. Brewster came instead."

"Oh." He chuckled. "I see. Tell me, did you really expect to see ghosts?"

"We wouldn't have gone otherwise," Bruce said tightly. "It was just an idea. I'm sorry Mrs. Brewster was annoyed. I don't know what she thought I was doing—body-snatching or something. I wish she would stop bothering me." He rose abruptly. "Excuse me. I'm not hungry."

"Bruce," Uncle Harold said quickly. Bruce paused, his hands closed on the back of his chair. "I don't question your methods in this case. But I should have thought you would have formed your conclusion about ghosts a few years earlier in your life."

"I thought I had." He turned. They heard his steps going down the hall quickly, toward the front door. Uncle Harold touched his eyes.

"I said something. What did I say?"

Carol pushed her chair. "I don't know. I'll be back; I'm starving. Aunt Catherine, your eggs are burning."

She caught up with Bruce as he went out the door, and he snapped miserably without stopping, "Why did you tell? Couldn't you think up a good lie or stay quiet so I could? Now he'll know I'm barmy, brainless as a six-year-old scared of monsters under his bed—"

Carol stopped in the doorway, flushed and silent. "I'm sorry."

He looked back at her. His shoulders slumped. He went back to the porch and dropped onto the step. "I'm sorry. I shouldn't have shouted at you. Why didn't you shout back at me? You always do."

She looked down at his bent head. "I don't know . . . I thought—the truth was as good as a lie, then."

He was silent a moment. "Well. You were right," he said softly. "That's a funny way to put it. I don't know where I was going, anyway. And it won't do any good, my going. I'll just have to come back. So I might as well stay here and think."

"I have an idea."

He turned. "What is it then?" he said hopefully.

"I was thinking. . . ." She sat down beside him on the cold porch. The shadow of the house flowed over them, over the pool, to the edge of the stone wall where the morning light had begun to warm the stones. "Priests think a lot about dead people. Father Malory might believe us."

V

THEY FOUND FATHER MALORY IN THE CHURCH, FOLD-
ing up music stands. He smiled at them as they came
up the aisle. The side windows were narrow, round-
arched, and the light fell in slender fingers from them
to touch the pews. The light from the great east window above the altar flamed from the glass rose and
turned Father Malory's face a gentle pink.

"Good morning," he said. "We've just had choir
practice."

"With Roger Simmons' cello?" Bruce said. "I saw
him leave."

"Oh, yes. And we have some guitars and Martin
Brewster's recorder. He wanted to play a guitar, but he
can't quite handle it and he keeps trying to sing. So I
found him something simpler. Randall Harris wanted
to bring his trombone, but he tends to drown out every-

one else. So I let him bring his flute, which sounds quite nice with the cello whenever they hit the right notes." He paused a moment, gathering music. "It's an odd combination, but they are so eager, and that counts. They haven't performed at a mass yet. I hope people will enjoy them."

"I hope so, too," Bruce said. "It sounds like a good idea. Father—" He broke off as Father Malory reached out and turned his face gently from the light.

"I didn't think that odd coloring was from the window. . . . I'm sorry. Go on. I interrupted you."

Bruce sighed. "I don't know how to say it."

"Start at the beginning and proceed logically."

"That sounds like something Dad would say."

"He did," Father Malory said.

"Ghosts," Carol said, "aren't logical."

Father Malory's eyes moved to her face. He shook the pile of music to straighten it, tapping it gently, rhythmically on a pew-back even after it had fallen into place. "I really don't know anything about ghosts," he said. "Why do you think they aren't logical?"

"Because if they were, they wouldn't walk through cellar walls."

Father Malory let the music rest for a moment on the pew-back. Then he dropped it on the seat and sat down. "I suppose that's true. I don't see why they should. Do they?"

"Yes."

His eyes moved back and forth across their faces. He

drew a deep breath. "How strange. Who are they, do you know?"

"We know one of them," Bruce said. "The girl in the painting in Dad's study. We just saw her yesterday. She came out of the sunlight in her blue dress and white collar, and she walked straight through Mrs. Brewster's cellar wall. No. Before she did, she turned and said, 'Edward. Come.' Then she walked into the wall."

79

Father Malory was silent. The church was silent about them, cool, dark in the far corners by the high round arch of the heavy oak door, where the light could not reach yet. His eyes moved from their faces; he stared at the rose window.

"Do you believe us?" Bruce said. Father Malory's eyes came back to him.

"Yes. But belief is not the same as knowledge." He sighed slightly. "I amaze myself at times."

"You amaze *me*," Bruce said. "If I told Dad what we—" He stopped abruptly.

"You haven't tried?"

"Oh, we've tried. But he can't—the problem is, he can't see them."

"Oh."

"And I'm not going to come straight out and tell him. He is interested in facts. Ghosts don't exist. That's fact. Well, I've seen two. That's another fact. I brought him down to the cellar one day after I'd seen the first one, and Dad couldn't see it. But Carol's seen both of them."

"Oh. . . ." He stirred, his eyes falling away from them again, glinting a little in the morning light. "Do you know what century that young girl's clothes belong to?"

"No."

"The same century the house as it stands now was built in. The seventeenth century. The century of Civil War, the Stuart Kings, of the beginnings of modern science, the beginnings of religious toleration. . . . You mentioned two ghosts. Who is the other?"

"He wears black," Bruce said. "He wears pants that come down to his knees and dark stockings and—"

"He looks like a Pilgrim," Carol said. "But he carries a sword in his hand."

"A sword." He fell silent. Then he straightened, rising. "I must go. I told old Mrs. Louis I could come visit this morning; she's in bed with a broken ankle. When can I come and see them with you?"

"I've always seen them about four." He hesitated. "Can you—can you come without my parents seeing you? I don't want to explain. Not until you've seen them. I'll wait for you in the yard."

"We can try, but I think. . . . Bruce, why don't you tell your father? Let him come down with us. He'll—"

"Can't you understand? He doesn't listen. Carol's told him twice there are ghosts in the cellar, and the minute he hears the word, you can tell that he's trying to think what she might have mistaken for a ghost. And I don't—I don't want him to think—he thinks I'm crazy enough as it is—I ride into blackberry hedges, I forget to come home for dinner, I argue with everybody and get into fights, and—last night we were in the graveyard waiting for ghosts, and Mrs. Brewster caught us, and Carol told him exactly what we were doing, and he looked at me like—like I was daft or the village idiot—and that's what I feel like sometimes,

81

when I talk to him. I don't feel like that talking to you."

Father Malory picked up the music and the music stands. They walked down the aisle with him. "Your father has a very clear, sensible mind and a generous personality. I think you could hurt him very deeply, if you wanted to."

Bruce stopped. Father Malory opened the door and looked back at him. The rounded doorway framed the long slope of green grass in front of the church that ran down the hill toward the busy street below. Carol's head turned from Bruce to Father Malory, her brows tugging together anxiously. Bruce's hands opened and closed.

"What makes you think I want that?"

"Because you do hurt him," Father Malory said simply. There was a step beyond the door; his head turned. "Oh, good morning, Mrs. Simpson. Have you come to wash the altar linen?"

Bruce passed them wordlessly. Carol caught up with him, hurrying a little to match his long, quick strides through the graveyard. His head was lowered; he did not notice Alexander blocking the path with his bicycle until Carol slowed beside him, and Alexander said, "Bruce. How's your eye?"

Bruce's head jerked up. Alexander rocked back and forth on the wheels in a fragile balance. His face was unusually quiet; when Bruce's quick steps did not check, he looked startled.

"Bruce—"

Bruce walked into his back wheel. He lost his balance as the bicycle overturned and fell, half-kneeling on the spokes, his hands smacking on the walk. Alexander lay half-under the bicycle, blinking and catching his breath. He turned slowly and pushed the handlebars from under his ribs. Bruce got up. He stepped across the wheel and went on without a word. Alexander untangled himself; Carol heard the faint shaking of his breath. He rolled to his feet, half-crouched, and with a sudden lunge, caught Bruce's legs and brought him down flat on the walk.

"Will you listen?" His voice was breathless, oddly sharp. "Do you think I wanted that to happen to you that day?" Bruce struggled beneath him; Alexander got up, and Bruce rolled over, his breath coming in short, painful catches. Blood trickled from a raw scrape on Alexander's elbow; he touched it and winced. "I wouldn't do that to you. I wouldn't. I happen to like pictures of cows and Queen Anne's Lace, but you wouldn't listen if I told you. You're not very good at listening." He limped to his bicycle. Bruce stared at him, his face pinched, white. He got to his feet. Alexander picked up his bicycle. He turned before he mounted, in time to see Bruce run down the walk, turn the corner toward the open field.

Alexander leaned against the railing. He looked at Carol. She stood gazing down the walk, her hands under her arms as though she were cold. Alexander sighed. "I have one of his pictures. The flowers. He nearly stepped on it, fighting, so I rescued it. If he wants it, tell him." He mounted stiffly. She watched him go. She went slowly down the path toward the house, and the bells struck a half-hour behind her. She went through the front door, standing open to warm the flagstones, and into the kitchen where Aunt Catherine measured flour for a cake.

"We're going to London tomorrow," she said cheerfully. "Harold decided he needed a holiday. What do you feel like doing?"

"Throwing all Mrs. Brewster's teacups against the wall."

"What's the matter?"

"Everything."

She waited alone in the afternoon, standing high in the tree by the gate, watching the field for Bruce. The bells rang a quarter to four, and she saw Father Malory walk down the graveyard path, his black suit speckled with sunlight from the windblown trees. She jumped down to meet him as he opened the gate.

"Hello, Carol," he said. "Where is Bruce?"

"I don't know. He ran away."

He stood quietly a moment, the wind tugging at his sleeves, raising tufts in his hair. He smoothed them down absently. "Will he come back?"

"I don't know. I think so. Are you still coming down?"

"Yes, of course."

"Then wait here a moment, and I'll see if the coast is clear." She stood in the doorway and listened. She heard the click of Uncle Harold's typewriter, and after a moment, Aunt Catherine's steps across the floor above her head. She beckoned to Father Malory, waiting patiently on the lawn, and he came to the door and followed her into the cellar. She cleared a place for him among Mrs. Brewster's what-nots, and he sat down on the table. A moment later the cellar door opened. They heard soft steps on the stones. Father Malory shifted uneasily on the table, and a little china shepherdess fell into a teacup behind him. He sat still. Then Bruce came through the doorway, and Father Malory sighed.

"I had a sudden vision," he murmured, "of you being Mrs. Brewster."

Bruce sat down on a pile of books. He said after a moment, "She would have to be polite to you." Then he blinked as a man moved between them in black cape and hat.

"I don't know why she would," Father Malory said meditatively. "Rules of etiquette don't cover the possibility of finding priests sitting among one's antiques in one's cellar."

The ghost turned, walked into the wall, and Bruce's eyes jumped to Father Malory's face. His mouth opened, closed again. Father Malory looked at him a moment. He looked at Carol, sitting beside him, her face turned to him, her mouth open, wordless.

85

"Did I miss something? I did, didn't I."

Bruce sighed. He stared at the floor, his shoulders slumped. A shadow fell over his face; a skirt rustled faint as the wind beyond the thick stones. A blue-eyed girl looked down at him.

"Edward," she said softly. "Come." And the stones she melted through reappeared firm and immovable behind her.

Carol slid off the table. Father Malory said surprisedly, "Is it over?"

"Yes. They came." She sat down suddenly on the floor, feeling the blood rushing to her face, a heaviness gathering in her throat. She put her head down on her knees; the first sob scraped her throat like a hiccup. "I wanted—I wanted you to see them—"

"Don't cry. Please don't cry."

"I feel like it." The tears ran hot to her chin; she rubbed her face against her knees to dry it. "Everything—nothing is going right—you could have told Uncle Harold you saw them, and then—and then Bruce wouldn't have to hate the house—and I don't know what to do with two ghosts nobody else can see; I don't know why they have to be there, and you'll think we're both barmy—"

"I don't think you're barmy," Father Malory said.

"I would if I were you." She felt a touch on her shoulder and lifted her head. Bruce knelt beside her, holding out a handkerchief. She took it and blew her nose.

"Just because everything is going wrong, that's no reason to give up," Bruce said.

"Well, I don't know what else to do."

"We'll think of what we should do, and then we'll do it. That's the only logical thing to do."

"You don't like thinking logically."

"Well sometimes—sometimes it's the only thing left to do. When you only have one thing left to do, you do it. But I don't think sitting on the floor and crying is going to help."

"Well, running away this morning didn't help any either."

He was silent a moment. "I know." He stood up, looking at Father Malory sitting silently on the table. "What are you going to do? Tell Dad?"

"No," Father Malory said reflectively. "It's your problem. I expect you'll find a way to solve it. I didn't see or hear anything unusual. But I did see your faces as you watched, and I have been listening to you, and I don't blame you for feeling frustrated. I feel a bit left out. I don't know why you should be able to see something so exciting when I can't. But I can offer one comforting thought: unless the girl had a habit of wandering about when she was alive in clothes two hundred years out of her time, whoever painted that picture saw her as a ghost."

"But he didn't paint her in the cellar," Bruce said. "There was an archway. And I can't see any place in the wall that looks like an arch has been filled up. The stones look like they've been solid for centuries."

Father Malory nodded, his eyes narrowed, search-ing the walls. "It is strange. . . ." He looked at his watch and stood up. They walked slowly back through the rooms. He stopped at the foot of the steps and said, "I wonder. Do you suppose that's what Susan saw in the cellar? She saw the girl from the painting walk through the cellar wall, and then she ran to the study and looked at the painting and had hysterics."

"Poor Susan," Carol said. Bruce looked at her.

"You saw the same thing, and you didn't have hys-terics."

"I would have," she said thoughtfully, "if I knew how." She opened the cellar door and peered out. The rich smell of fried chicken hung in the passage. They came out and closed the door softly, just as Uncle Har-old came out of the study, his pipe in his mouth and paper in his hand.

"Cath—Father Malory! I didn't know you were here."

"I wasn't."

"You're just the person I need. I have been writing all afternoon, and suddenly nothing I have written makes any sense whatsoever—Can you spare me a moment?"

He led Father Malory to the study. Bruce stood watching them until the study door closed behind them. He stuck his hands deep in his pockets and looked at Carol.

"Have you got any ideas?"

"I had the last idea. It's your turn."

He looked down at the floor. "I don't think I'm thinking too well today," he said. "I wish my bicycle were fixed. . . . I would ride so far away that by the time I came back I wouldn't even remember all the things that happened today." He turned away, going down the hall to the kitchen. "Oh, well. At least there's fried chicken."

"And we're going to London tomorrow."

"Are we?"

"Is that far enough?"

His face tugged into a smile. "It might help. We'll probably see all the ghosts of the kings of England walking in and out of walls."

They saw the long line of the kings and queens of England standing waxen and ghostly in a museum in the middle of London the next day.

"They aren't moving," Carol said. Her voice was hushed. The museum was filled with wax people who stared at them, silent and aloof from other ages, caught forever in some intense memory of their lives. Uncle Harold and Aunt Catherine strolled ahead, unconcerned beneath the regal eyes of dead kings. Bruce flicked through the pages of the guidebook.

"Richard III. That's who comes after Edward V. I never can remember."

"What happened to Henry VII?"

"He's down a bit—that man with the long fur coat. And then there's—"

"Henry VIII. I know him." She stopped before him and he surveyed her glassily, his brows proudly arched. "He had six wives, and he chopped their heads off when he got tired of them."

"Not all of them—some of them just died. That's Queen Elizabeth with the red hair. She liked to win arguments, too."

"What do you mean 'too'?" Carol asked suspiciously, but he had moved on to a slender gentleman with a little pointed beard.

"That's Charles I. He got his head chopped off."

"I didn't know you were allowed to chop kings' heads off."

"There was a war." He stopped, his eyes narrowed a little, as though he were trying to remember something. "The Civil War. He lost his head, and after him came—"

"Charles II?"

"No. Cromwell."

"He's not in the guidebook."

"He wasn't a king. He was a Puritan."

"I thought the Puritans all left England and went to Massachusetts."

He shook his head. "They were very strong followers of Cromwell during the Civil War. They didn't like churches with stained-glass windows and bell-towers and statues, and they destroyed a lot of them during the war. They also didn't like the way Charles I was ruling. So they had a war in 1642 and chopped his head off in 1649, and put Cromwell in to rule. But when Cromwell died and his son began to rule, they decided anything else was better than him, and they asked Charles II to come back."

"That was a good bird's-eye view of the first half of the seventeenth century," Uncle Harold said behind him, and they turned. "Well, are you about finished?"

"Dad, we haven't even seen the Chamber of Horrors yet," Bruce said. "We got stuck on the Stuart Kings."

"Oh, by all means," Uncle Harold said. "Take your time." He tucked Aunt Catherine's hand under his arm. "I'll go and commune with the famous statesmen."

"What is the Chamber of Horrors?" Carol said, looking over Bruce's shoulder as he turned pages.

"It's full of murderers, criminals . . . old-fashioned tortures. . . ." His voice died away. He stood frowning down at the guidebook, and for a moment Carol did not even hear him breathe. "Carol—"

"What is it?"

"Look at that man in the picture."

"Hold still, I can't—Oh. . . ." Her fingers closed tightly on his wrist as she stared at the pale grim face half-hidden under his thumb. Her voice rose in a wail. "He's a ghost—what's he doing in the Chamber of Horrors?"

"Sh! He's not in the Chamber of Horrors." He looked around. "Come on. This way."

Carol followed him out of the room. They saw the man again, one of a group of people in a motionless wax tableau. They stopped in front of it. Five men sat at a table. Their hats and clothes were dark; there was no lace on their plain white collars and cuffs. A small boy stood before them on a footstool. His hair was bright in the somber room. There were bows on his shoes and round his knees. His collar was peaked with points of lace. Behind him a portly man wearing a helm and a breastplate of steel quieted three anxious women whose rich clothes seemed to draw the light away from the darkly dressed men.

"It's not him," Carol said softly.

"But it could be."

"It's not."

"That's not the point. . . . Carol, those men are dressed exactly like the ghost was—and the girl has that same kind of white lace collar, and her hair comes down in curls like that woman's—she's from their time."

Carol stared at them. They were frozen in some elusive, unexplained moment. "What are they doing?"

" 'When Did You Last See Your Father?' It's a reproduction of a painting."

"I don't get it."

"I don't—" He lifted his head, looking down the room. "Dad."

Uncle Harold left Mary Queen of Scots kneeling with her head on a chopping-block and came to them. "Problem?"

"Yes. What is happening here?"

"Oh. It's quite simple. The men in black are Puritan leaders. They are looking for the boy's father, who is evidently a Royalist leader, because if he were a good staunch Puritan, he wouldn't let his family wear such rich colorful clothes. One of the women is probably the boy's mother."

"Would that be during the Civil War?"

"During it, or shortly after it, I expect. The Puritans seem to be definitely in power."

"Dad. That painting in your study—this reminds me of it."

Uncle Harold glanced at him. "I didn't know you had looked that closely at it."

"Yes. I like it."

"So do I. The dress seems to be of the same period, doesn't it. Perhaps she was looking for her father, too. She always seemed to me to be looking for someone. . . . I wonder where your mother is. I think I left her in the Chamber of Horrors."

"I'm here," Aunt Catherine said. "And I am starving. Intellectual pursuits always have that effect on me."

"But Dad," Bruce said, "we haven't seen the Chamber of Horrors yet."

They were finally ready to leave, when Carol saw

93

the wax statue of a small old woman in black, with spectacles on her nose and a fringed shawl about her shoulders. She looked oddly out of place among the richly dressed dignitaries of past ages.

"Who is that?"

Uncle Harold smiled. "That is Madame Tussaud. She made that statue of herself over a hundred years ago. It was she who made the first statues for this museum."

They had supper, and then Uncle Harold took them to a play. The play had a prince dressed in mournful black who saw an armed ghost, and the ghost spoke of foul murder by poison and would not stay past dawn. Carol watched quietly until the ghost vanished; then she leaned over and whispered in Bruce's ear, "Maybe the man with the sword murdered Edward."

"Sh." After a moment he whispered back, "Maybe Edward killed the man with the sword."

"Maybe the girl—"

"Sh—" said someone behind, and they quieted.

"One may smile and smile," said the prince, "and be a villain."

The play ended with his death. Soldiers came to carry his dead body off-stage, and then the lights went on, and people clapped, and he came back on his own feet, smiling and bowing. Carol looked at Bruce.

"Do you remember the part where Hamlet was with his mother, and he saw the ghost, but his mother couldn't see it?"

"It's only a play."

"I know, but it happened to him. And it happened to us. I wonder why ghosts do that."

Bruce yawned. "I don't know. I expect he was imagining the whole thing."

"He was not." She stood up and followed Uncle Harold out.

"Did you enjoy it?" he said.

"Yes. But I didn't expect everyone to die in the end."

Uncle Harold found the car keys and unlocked the car. "In Shakespeare's day they rather enjoyed stages full of dead bodies."

"Well I enjoyed it, too. But it was still sad."

They drove around the city the next day and visited great ancient buildings with a bewildering array of names: the Tower of London, the Houses of Parliament, Buckingham Palace. When they got to Westminster Cathedral, their feet began to hurt. Carol looked at it, shifting from one foot to another. It was a vast building, striped red and white, with round arched windows, and domes, and many-sided towers. "It's so big. . . ." Carol said. It ran the length of the city block. Uncle Harold laughed.

"All right. It can wait for another trip. You've seen enough tombs for one day."

They had some lunch, and then started back. Carol slept most of the way. She woke finally and saw in the distance a small town of grey stone houses and outlying farms and a church on a hill in the middle of it, the grey spire rising clear of the trees.

"We're home," Uncle Harold said cheerfully. And beside Carol, Bruce slouched lower in the seat, his hands in his pockets, and she heard the slow whisper of his sigh.

VI

A GREEN VAN HAD TAKEN UNCLE HAROLD'S PARKING place in front of the gate.

"What on earth—" Uncle Harold said. He parked behind it. The closed doors of the van said in bright orange letters: MIDDLETON CIVIL SEWAGE. "Is something wrong with our plumbing?"

"Perhaps someone broke a water pipe," Aunt Catherine said. "I don't think the city would be interested in our plumbing."

They got out and collected suitcases from the trunk. Two men stood at the edge of the field where the road ended and watched them. Uncle Harold went over to talk to them. The church bells rang the half-hour. Bruce looked at his watch.

"What time is it? My watch stopped."

"Four-thirty," Aunt Catherine said. "Bruce, will you

take your father's suitcase in, please. Hello, Emily."

"Hello, my dear," Emily Raison said. "Did you have a nice stay?"

"Yes, it was very nice. What are the plumbers doing here?"

"Oh, my dear, we're in for a bit of noise. They're going to put a drain in the street."

"A drain? What for? Nobody's drowned yet in this neighborhood, and it's been here for centuries."

"They say the street slants, and all the rain goes into the field, and it makes the field muddy when they want to practice soccer. We've had a lot of rain this summer, you know. Bless me—Bruce, what did you do to your poor face?"

"I fell in a blackbery bush," Bruce said patiently.

"Oh, it looks terrible. You're so lucky you still have your eyes. My Uncle Herbert had to have a glass eye when he ran into a nail in a fence. But he was poaching." She turned back to Aunt Catherine. "Well, my dear, I expect you want to go in and have a nice hot cup of tea after that long drive."

"And a footstool under each foot," Aunt Catherine said. "Only Harold has the house keys."

Carol sat down on her suitcase. Uncle Harold came back and she stood up.

"Do you know what they're going to do?" he said indignantly.

"Yes. Emily told us."

"I've never heard anything so ridiculous. They'd

make a man's home unfit for living in for two weeks, just so they can get rid of a few mud puddles."

"I know," Aunt Catherine said soothingly. "You'd think they never heard of rubbers."

"I won't be able to write a word."

"I know."

"I won't be able to think!"

"Maybe you could find something else to do for a while. Meanwhile, if I don't get off my blistered feet, you're going to have to carry me over the threshold, suitcase and all."

"Oh." He looked down at the keys in his hand. "I was wondering why you were all standing out here. I'm sorry. Shall I go down later for fish and chips? It will save you cooking."

She smiled. "That would be lovely."

Carol sat in her window-seat after dinner, with a postcard of the Tower of London on the windowsill in front of her. She frowned over it, nibbling on her pen. Finally she wrote "Dear Mom and Dad," and somebody knocked on her door.

"Carol?"

"Come in."

Bruce came in. She moved her feet, and he sat down beside her on the window-seat.

"What are you doing?"

"I'm writing a postcard. I can't think of anything to say. Nothing I think of makes any sense. Dear Mother. How are you? I am fine. England is very nice, only they have problems with ghosts and drains—"

He laughed. He twisted himself around and stared out of the open window, his chin resting on one fist.

"I just wanted to think, and I thought it might be easier to do it out loud."

She nodded. "I've been trying to think, too, only it isn't doing much good."

"What we've got is two ghosts left over from the Civil War period walking through a wall. It doesn't make any sense. The man must be a Puritan. And the girl doesn't look like she is—she's too pretty."

"Some Puritans probably were pretty. They couldn't help it."

"You know what I mean—her hair is in curls, and her dress is the same color as her eyes are, and her shoes have fake roses in them."

Carol's head turned slowly. "Her dress is the same color her eyes are?"

"Cobalt blue. Didn't you notice? We could have a worse-looking ghost to worry about—she doesn't have fangs or a wart on her nose, and if she appeared by your bed at night you'd only have a mild attack. Anyway, she probably isn't a Puritan. So why are they in the same cellar?"

"They're both waiting for Edward."

"Who is Edward? And where is he? If we can see them, why can't we see Edward?"

"Why should we see either one of them? They've been dead for centuries. What good does it do for ghosts to hang around after they're dead?"

"Maybe they got stuck in time, doing one thing over and over again, like a broken record playing the same thing over and over."

"Well, why can't Father Malory and Uncle Harold see them, if they're stuck? Why does it have to be us?"

"I don't know."

They were silent. Below them, the fishpond was a grey still shadow in the gathering dusk.

Bruce said, "She doesn't say much. I wonder if she knows we're there. There are times when it seems she's looking straight at you, until you remember she's a ghost, and she can't see you . . . or can she?" He shook his head. "We'll never figure anything out until we can find out why they go through that wall. I'm tempted to tear it down, except I'd never be able to explain to Dad if there's nothing behind it. And I don't see what could possibly be there."

"Edward is a Royalist leader. The man with the sword is a Puritan leader. He wants to capture Edward. The girl is trying to help Edward hide."

"Behind a brick wall? And where is Edward? When she says 'Edward. Come,' why doesn't he come?"

"She's talking to us, then. We're supposed to come."

"How?"

Carol puffed her cheeks and sighed. "Maybe Edward was a pirate, and there's a buried treasure behind the wall, and he and the man with the sword fought over it and the girl. . . ."

"Yes—what about the girl?"

"I'll think of something. Anyway the man killed Edward, stole the gold, and locked Edward's bones in the treasure-chest, and that's why we never see him."

"Ghosts don't need bones. If they can get out of coffins, they can get out of treasure-chests. And why would a pirate bury a treasure so far inland?"

"I don't know."

"There must have been something behind that wall. But what?"

"Another room?"

"There's no trace of another room. And if there was one, why would they have sealed it off? People don't usually build cellars that extend farther than the house."

"What about a hiding place for Royalist leaders?"

He smiled. "We're going round and round, like squirrels in one of those moving tracks they put in cages. It seems logical that Edward was a Royalist leader, and she might be trying to hide him. But I don't know how she did it without knocking the wall down, and there's not much sense in that; you can hide a man more easily than you can hide the evidence that you've knocked down a wall to make a hiding place. And somebody put the wall back up—if it was ever down. I don't know." He rubbed his eyes. "Let's talk about something else awhile and maybe we'll think of something accidentally."

"All right. Alexander has your picture of the flowers. He said he likes it, but he'll give it back to you if you want it."

In the fading light, she saw his face flush scarlet. He made a sudden movement as if he were going to rise, but instead he sat quietly, staring out the window. He was silent for a long while. She picked up the postcard and frowned at it. She began to write. He stirred finally.

"Did you think of something to say?"

"Finally. How do you spell Madame Tussaud?"

He spelled it for her. Then he said, "Perhaps you are right. Perhaps the girl was trying to hide Edward from the Puritans and the man with the sword found his hiding place. . . . Perhaps Edward was someone she loved—her brother, or—no, she's too young to

103

have a husband. It was someone—her brother or a cousin or a friend, that she cared about, and she saw him killed and that's what keeps her coming back—her sadness. She keeps living it all over again."

The next day, during breakfast, the drilling began. It was not loud, but its dull, monotonous persistence wore away the tranquility of the morning. Uncle Harold endured it with patience, sipping his tea.

"In any society," he said, "there is bound to be a conflict between the people who want to write history, and those who want to drill drains for soccer players underneath their windows. There must be a happy meeting-point somewhere, but in this case I think I will yield and go work in the Cambridge library."

"Oh, good," Aunt Catherine said. "I'll go with you and do some shopping."

"Dad," said Bruce.

"Yes."

"I was—I was wondering. Do you have something I could do to earn money? I need tires for my bike and new paint, and all I've got is nine pence."

Uncle Harold looked at him silently a moment. He put his cup down. "You want to work?"

Bruce flushed. "Yes. Please."

"I'm sorry. I didn't mean it to sound that way. I was just wondering this morning what we were going to do for a gardener for the next two weeks, and here you are, practically begging to mow the lawns and clip the hedges once a week."

Bruce grimaced. But he said, "What happened to the gardener?"

"He's getting married to Miss Morris."

"Miss Morris? At the sweet shop?"

"Yes."

"She's an old lady."

"She is forty-three," Uncle Harold said with dignity. "Remind me to order my coffin at that age. I'll pay you what I pay the gardener—a pound a week. I had thought of doing it myself, but that side lawn looks too formidable for my old bones."

"It looks formidable for mine," Bruce said. "But I'll do it. Thanks, Dad." He rose, finishing his orange juice on the way up. "I'll work on the hedges this morning; there's no sense in cutting the grass before it needs it."

Carol found him later, after she finished breakfast. He was trimming the hedge by the gate. The wind, high that day, snatched the pieces as they fell from the clippers and rolled them down the walk. He put the clippers down a moment and flexed his fingers.

"Hello. Where are you going?"

"I'm taking this pan back to Emily Raison. She gave Aunt Catherine some tea in it the day I heated the stove up, and Aunt Catherine forgot to give it back." She swung the pan in an arc that flashed silver in the sunlight. "It's a nice day. Maybe I'll go for a walk." The drilling started up suddenly behind the gate, screaming into the silence, and she winced. "It sounds like a dentist's drill."

"Mm. Go across the field, and you can get out of town to the farms."

"Maybe I'll do that."

She opened the gate. Two men with drills and a truck stood between her and Emily Raison's house. She went toward the field to get around them, and when she got to the field—a great circle of green grass sloping gently toward a far road—the wind nudged her in the direction of other fields flowing on and on toward a flat horizon. The drilling grew faint behind her as she walked, until she could barely hear it. She swung the pan aimlessly in circles and smelled the grass, uncut, between her toes. She crossed the road and turned down a quiet highway with blackberry hedges enclosing fields. A fence took the place of the hedges farther down, and she stood on the bottom rail and watched a pair of thick-hooved farm horses cropping beneath the endless sky. In the next field a huge bull stuck his head through the fence and eyed her inscrutably. She circled gingerly around him. She picked a thick handful of buttercup, white Queen Anne's Lace, blue morning glory streaked with white. The flat midlands ran serene and changeless to the end of the world, and the occasional car that whisked by seemed alien and transitory.

She came back an hour later and went through the gate before she remembered Emily Raison's pan. She stood a moment, looking at the hedge, puzzled. The clippers lay on the clippings in the wheelbarrow, and only about five feet of the hedge was trimmed. She looked around, but she did not see Bruce. She went into the street. Uncle Harold's car was gone. She scratched her head absently a moment, then went over to Emily Raison's house and saw her in the graveyard weeding graves.

She opened the gate and went into the graveyard. Miss Emily smiled vaguely at her.

"Hello, my dear. What lovely buttercups."

"How many graves are you going to clean?"

"Oh, I'm just doing a bit of weeding over Mr. Chapman. He was a good friend of the family when I was a little girl."

Carol knelt down beside her. "Homer Chapman. 1861–1920. He's next door to Elizabeth Greyson." She picked a straggling piece of moss off Elizabeth Greyson's stone.

"Is he, then?" Miss Emily said comfortably.

"It's so old . . . 1599–1643. . . . She was buried here over three hundred years ago . . . three hundred years, and her gravestone is still standing up straight, and the church she was buried beside is still standing. . . . They made things to last in those days." She stepped across Elizabeth's grave. "And here's her husband, Jonathon."

"Is he, then?"

"And they had a child, buried here." She knelt down again and coaxed a snail off one of the letters.

Slugs had left silver trails like glistening tears across the stone. "Thomas, son of Elizabeth and Jonathon Greyson." She brushed apart the grass and weed in front of the stone. "It says something. . . . 'You are. . . . You are a priest forever, according to the order of Mel—Mel—something. Melchisedech.' Who is Melchisedech?"

"I don't know, my dear. Some of the people here were before my time."

"He was 1616 to 1644. 1642 was the Civil War. He was a priest in the middle of the Civil War. I wonder if that's what killed him. I wonder if he got captured by the Puritans."

"Then he should have gone through the priest tunnel," Miss Emily said. "He would have been safe."

"What's a priest tunnel?"

"Oh, my dear, they had a nice tunnel between the church and the house so priests could move from one place to another without being caught." She flung a handful of weed into the wind. Carol stared at her, hugging her knees. She could feel her heart thumping against her knees.

"Who did? Who had a tunnel?"

"The people who lived in the house then." She sat back on her heels and brushed her hands off. "Bless me. I'm all grass-stained."

Carol stood up and walked across the graves. She squatted down beside Miss Emily. "What kind of a tunnel? Where does it begin?"

"I don't know. Nobody has ever seen it. I heard Mrs. Brewster's father talk of it. Mrs. Brewster has looked for herself, but she could never find it. So she says it's only a legend; that there's no such thing as a priest tunnel. But I say: who began the legend? The people who built the tunnel, that's who."

Carol sat down on the grass. "A tunnel," she whispered. "A tunnel. . . . Would it go underneath the graveyard?"

"Oh, it went right under the church. That's what I've heard. Is that my saucepan?"

"Oh. Yes." She handed it to Miss Emily. "Aunt Catherine says thanks." She sat quietly, wind blowing the hair across her face. She laughed suddenly, breathlessly, and brushed it away, feeling her fingers cold against her face. "A tunnel. I wonder if it's still there."

"There's no knowing that," Miss Emily said, searching in the earth for the end of a dandelion root. "It may have fallen in."

"Maybe. But everything else has lasted." She stood up. Miss Emily looked up at her.

"Would you like some milk and a biscuit, my dear?"

"No thanks. I have to talk to Bruce." She hoisted herself up on the railing and dropped over, and ran across the street, scarcely seeing the trucks and the drills. She opened the gate. The hedge-clippers were in the wheelbarrow, and Bruce was nowhere to be seen.

The workers left at four-thirty, and he still had not returned. Uncle Harold and Aunt Catherine drove up shortly afterward. Carol watched them from her window. They parked at the end of the graveyard to avoid the work area, and walked half the block. She saw Uncle Harold stop in mid-sentence when he saw the wheelbarrow, and then she went down to open the door for them.

"Hello, Carol. Where is Bruce?" he said as he came in.

"I don't know."

"Well. I didn't realize you would have to stay by yourself all day. We should have taken you with us to see the University."

"I didn't mind. I went for a walk."

"Hello," Bruce said behind them, and they turned. Alexander smiled cheerfully beside him.

"Hello."

Uncle Harold felt for his pipe. His mouth tugged in a smile as he lit it. "Alexander. What have you been doing with yourself?"

"Being lazy. I came to take a look at Bruce's bicycle."

"You came on foot?"

"I have a small problem with my back spokes." His slow, calm voice was changeless. "I thought I should do a bit of walking before I forget how. Tomorrow I might even try running. How's your article?"

"I think I may have to finish it in Edinburgh." He looked at Carol. "How does a couple weeks of camping in Scotland sound to you?"

She sat down on the stairs. "Scotland? I don't—I don't even know what it's like."

"You'll like it," Bruce said. "There are dark green hills, miles of them, with sheep feeding on them, and the ruins of old stone walls running up and down them. It's beautiful."

"It sounds beautiful. I've never camped before."

"That," Aunt Catherine said, "is a different proposition entirely. You get up in a faint drizzle in the mornings to drink lukewarm tea, after chasing spiders out of your cold bed—"

"A little rain never hurt anybody," Bruce said. He stopped. His eyes flickered to Uncle Harold's face. "I put the tools away, in case it decides to rain overnight. I didn't mean to be gone all day."

Uncle Harold shook his head surprisedly. "It's all right." He took his papers and books into the study.

Aunt Catherine said, "I suppose I should feed you. Alexander, you're welcome to supper, if you don't mind taking a chance." She went upstairs with her packages. Bruce looked at Carol.

"What's the matter? You're so quiet."

"I've got an idea." Her voice shook in spite of herself. She glanced at Alexander, lounging against the banister, and he straightened.

"Don't you want me to hear?" he said wistfully. "I like ideas."

She looked doubtfully at Bruce, but his eyes were on Alexander's face. Then he dropped beside her.

"Go ahead. Just say it."

"All right. Emily Raison says they built a tunnel during the Civil War for priests to move from the house to the church without getting caught."

"A tunnel. . . ." he breathed.

"A priest tunnel."

He stared at her without seeing her. Then his face broke into a slow grin of pure joy.

"A tunnel!" he shouted, and clapped his hands over his mouth. Alexander dropped on one knee before them.

"Oh, please." His hands were clasped in petition. "Oh, please. I've always wanted an underground tunnel. Tell me what's happening."

Bruce stood up, nudging him off-balance. "Get up before Dad hears. Come on—" They followed him into the front yard and sat by the fishpool.

Bruce said, "Tell me what Emily said."

"She said it was a legend, about the tunnel. She said Mrs. Brewster had looked for it, but she couldn't find it, so she said it didn't really exist—it was only a story. But Bruce, Edward could have been escaping through the tunnel. And the girl was going to lead him through it. But the man was waiting there for him. I don't know what happens after that—he might have captured Edward or maybe Edward captured him. But it does explain why they keep walking through the wall, as though there were a door there . . . or an arch. . . ."

Bruce drew a deep breath. He stared into the pool, his eyes wide, dark with thought. "And we know exactly where it is."

"If it's still there. If it ever was there."

"Something was there, unless they're just walking through a wall for the fun of it. And if we do find the tunnel or the remains of it, that will be proof of what we've seen."

"Bruce," said Alexander. "Bruce, what are you talking about? Who is Edward? Who keeps walking through walls?"

"The girl in the painting in my Dad's study," Bruce said. "And a man with a sword. They keep walking through our cellar wall."

Alexander's mouth opened. It closed slowly, then opened again. His voice came finally, hushed. "You have ghosts in your cellar, and you kept them all to yourself. Of all the rotten, selfish—And now you've got a tunnel, too."

"Mrs. Brewster has a tunnel. Or she's going to."

"I wanted to tell you," Carol said. "But you don't believe in ghosts."

"Of course I don't. Who does? I didn't believe Bruce could draw cows, either, or do something as incredibly stupid as diving into a blackberry bush, but I've learned, haven't I? There's always room for learning. Knowledge is a sacred, never-dying flame, and that's what Mrs. Brewster is going to breathe if you tear her wall apart—fire and smoke like a dragon. I want to be there when she does. Bruce, if you don't let me help, I'll pine away at your doorstep and haunt it."

Bruce chuckled. But there was a worried line above his eyes. He dropped his fingers over the pool's edge and let the goldfish nibble at them. "I think we should," he said finally. "At any rate, I'm going to." He moved, and the goldfish started away, filling the pool with ring upon ring of widening ripples. "I don't think Mrs. Brewster will mind if we're right. But if we're wrong, and Dad finds out, and we have to tell him about ghosts he can't see and tunnels that aren't there. . . ." He shook his head, lifting his wet hand to rub his eyes. "I don't even want to think about it."

Alexander, watching him quietly, shifted on the grass. He picked a tiny blue flower absently and stared at it. "Bruce—"

There was an odd note in his voice. Bruce looked up. "What?"

Alexander was silent. He tossed the flower away and smiled his slow, imperturbable smile. There was a trace of color in his face. "Nothing. Are these private ghosts, or can anybody see them?"

"Dad can't. And Father Malory can't. Carol and I can, and I think whoever painted the picture of the girl saw her, and possibly a maid in the house when Mrs. Brewster was young. At any rate, she ran up from the cellar one day and looked at the picture and had hysterics."

"Why? The girl looks harmless."

114

"I know, but it's a bit startling when she walks through the wall."

"You didn't have hysterics, did you, Carol?" Alexander asked.

"No. I just ran."

"I promise I won't scream." His eyes crinkled in a smile. "Ghosts. If you're going to Scotland next week, we'd better get started."

"Mm. Tomorrow."

"There will be noise from our chisels. What will we do with it?"

"I don't know. It's right under Dad's study. . . ." He smiled slowly, his eyes glittering a little in the light from the study window. "He won't hear it. He won't hear a single tink from our chisels. Because all he'll be hearing tomorrow and the next day and the day after, is the Middleton Civil Sewage men drilling a hole in Parchment Street."

VII

THEY COULD HEAR THE WHINE OF THE DRILLING FAINT
and steady from the cellar the next morning. Over-
head they could hear Uncle Harold's footsteps as he
moved across the study. The stones were chilly; the
sun was warming the back of the house, and the front
lawn lay in shadow. Alexander stared at the solid wall.

"Where?"

"Under the window," Bruce said. He looked at
Carol and she nodded.

"Straight under."

Alexander put his hammer and chisel on the table.
He ran his fingers along a crack in the mortar, but it
was only a few inches long. He whistled softly.

"It's no wonder Mrs. Brewster never found it. I
say, when she asks you how you knew it was there,
what are you going to tell her?"

"I don't know. I haven't thought up a good lie yet." He steadied his chisel in the crack Alexander had investigated and gave it a solid thump with the hammer. A chip of mortar flew out. "She'd never believe the truth. Are you just going to stand there?"

"It looks solid. Perhaps I should go borrow some explosives."

"We'd have Uncle Harold dropping in on us," Carol said. She began working on the other end of Bruce's stone. "Maybe we should just take one out first. Then we can see what's behind it, and if there's just dirt, we can put it back."

"We can glue it back in," Alexander said. "Shove over and let me have a corner."

"It would look funny," Bruce said, "just sitting there without any mortar. But better one stone than three. One will take awhile anyway—this one looks about a foot deep." He lowered his arms a moment, flexing his fingers. His face was speckled with ancient mortar. He stared doubtfully at the wall.

"Think of Christopher Columbus discovering America," Alexander said, his voice breaking with the powerful, rhythmic blows of his hammer. "Think of Marco Polo discovering China. Think of—"

"Think of my mother coming down to put something in the freezer and discovering us."

"Let's not think," Carol said.

When the drilling stopped at noon, they had chipped the mortar as far as they could reach, and their chisels almost disappeared in the crevice that had formed around the stone. The noon bells drifted sweetly across the silence. They dropped their arms and slid to the floor.

"We'll have to find something longer," Bruce said. His bones cracked as he straightened his arms. "Spikes or something. I'll look in the tool-shed. Your faces are all white. Carol, your hair turned white."

"That's all right," she said tiredly. "I never liked it red."

"Why? It's a beautiful color. Vermilion, with touches of yellow ochre."

She looked at him out of the corners of her eyes. "It sounds like a disease."

"Red-gold," Alexander said, yawning. "If you're going to compliment somebody, you should do it in English."

"That wasn't a compliment. It was just a fact." He got to his feet and began to brush himself. "Come on. Let's go find some lunch."

Aunt Catherine was making sandwiches in the kitchen when they came in.

"Hello. What have you been up to?" She gave Carol a sandwich on a plate. Then she frowned puzzledly and brushed lightly at Carol's hair.

"We've been investigating," Alexander said.

"What? A chalk factory?" She opened the kitchen door and called down the hall, "Harold! Lunch!" They heard Uncle Harold's shout back. She turned and said irritably, "Bruce, will you sit down and give your food a fighting chance?"

Bruce sat down, chewing. They were silent, staring at their plates as they ate, until Alexander said, "That was good. May I have another?"

Bruce stood up. "I'll go to the tool-shed and get what we need."

"What are you doing?" Aunt Catherine said as he left. Alexander disposed of a quarter of his sandwich in a bite.

"Investigating antique stones," he said finally. "It's sort of archeology with a bit of geology thrown in. Like a fossil-hunt. We needed some chisels."

"Oh."

Uncle Harold came in. "What were you shouting? Oh—food. Good." He took a sandwich and peered into it. "Peanut butter?"

"Mine," said Aunt Catherine, rescuing it. She gave him another. "Yours."

"Is this lunch, or a lesson in possessive pronouns?"

The back door closed softly. Bruce passed them quickly, rather stiffly. Carol went out and joined him. He opened the cellar door quietly. She looked at what he was carrying.

"Isn't that a crowbar?"

"Sh. I thought we might need it. I got some long files and a big screwdriver—they should reach."

Alexander joined them a few minutes later. They waited until the drilling started again, and then they worked steadily all afternoon. The mortar chips filled the space they had opened, and white dust filmed their faces when they tried to blow it out. They got in each other's way and scraped mortar in each other's hair, and the space around the stone grew deeper and deeper. It seemed to hang suspended in its place in a mortar of air. Alexander stopped finally, after a long silent attack. He rubbed his face on his sleeve, and sweat and dust made a paste on his shirt.

"There's an end to it somewhere. Everything has an end. I was thinking: when it finally becomes unglued, we should have something underneath it—cardboard or a thin board—so we can pull it out more easily. Preferably something on wheels. Though I don't know yet how we're going to lift it down, once we've got it loose."

Bruce looked around vaguely. His face was a stiff white mask. "I'll flatten one of Mrs. Brewster's book boxes." He dropped his tools and stretched. Carol sat down on the floor and leaned her head against the stones. The drilling sounded monotonous and familiar as the buzzing of an insect. Bruce began to unpack one of the boxes beneath the table, his hands moving as though he were half-asleep. The church bells tolled the hour.

"Four o'clock," Alexander said. He yawned. "Four hours without a—" His voice stopped. They heard the clink of his tools on the stone.

A man stood beside him with a drawn sword in his

120

hand. His head turned as though he had heard a sound; his grim eyes rested briefly on Alexander's face. Alexander stared back at him, expressionless, motionless. Then, an instant before the man turned toward him, he jerked himself away in one quick turn. The man passed through the stones where he had stood.

"You saw him—" Carol whispered.

Alexander sat down beside her. She heard the shaking of his breath. "He would have walked straight through me—through my private bones—" He ran his hands down his face. "Blimey, there's another one—"

The girl came toward him through the sunlight, her skirt whispering softly in the silence. She turned before she reached the stones and looked down at Alexander.

"Edward. Come," she said. And then she walked through the wall, her collar melting into the stone they had been chipping loose. As she passed, the front of the stone settled downward with a small decisive thud.

Alexander closed his mouth. He looked at Carol wordlessly. Then he looked at Bruce.

"Did you see that?"

"Yes."

"I'm glad. When was the first time you saw them?"

"Last winter, sometime after we moved in—I don't remember exactly when—I saw the man. I didn't wait to see the girl."

"And nobody else saw him until Carol came? Nobody knew he was there but you? You never told anyone?"

"No." He took a stack of books out of the box. He shrugged slightly. "I thought—I didn't know what to think. Then Carol came and she saw him, too, and then finally we saw the girl, and things began to fall into place. And now you've seen her."

"And she's seen me."

"It looked like it."

"I think," Carol said, "she's like you. She doesn't trust older people."

Bruce took the last book out of the box. He got a penknife out of his pocket and began to cut down the corners. "It's hard to know," he said finally. He lifted his head. "Rot. The drilling stopped. I wanted to get that stone out today."

Alexander went to the wall. He probed at the mortar with a file. "It's cracked, I think, but it's still holding the stone. Maybe they'll start drilling again." He cleared a space on Mrs. Brewster's table and sat on it, watching Bruce flatten the box. "All that time we were terrorizing the peaceful country town of Middleton on our bicycles, you were sneaking off on the sly seeing ghosts and drawing flowers. It's amazing, what you don't know about people. . . . I wonder what Sandy Sparks does when he's not being generally ugly. Or Roger Simmons, when he's not crying. Do you suppose Sandy ever buys flowers for his mother?"

Bruce grinned. "Not bloody likely." He turned the box and started on another corner.

"Or Carol," Alexander said. "What do you suppose she does when nobody's looking?"

Bruce glanced at her. "She goes to bed with antique bed-warmers. And she hangs about a lot in trees. And she worries."

"How do you know?" Carol asked.

"You bite your fingernails. I notice. You have nice hands. They have good bones. You should try worrying without biting your nails."

She looked down at them doubtfully. "It's hard."

Bruce cut down the last corner. "What do you do when nobody's looking, Alexander? Write poetry?"

There was a small silence. "Me? The only sane member of the Middleton street gang?" He shifted on the table, and fragile glassware clinked together. There was a rich note of laughter in his voice. Bruce looked up at him. Alexander's face was scarlet.

Bruce slipped back on his heels. Alexander shifted again under his amazed stare, and a stack of saucers rattled warningly.

"You don't really. Do you, really?"

"It—it comes to that, when you like—the way words sound. Please, if you're going to laugh, get it over with so I can decide whether to throw a plate or just leave in dignity."

Bruce drew a deep breath. "I'm not going to laugh," he said dazedly.

"I don't think it's funny," Carol said. "I wish I could do that instead of hanging in trees."

"You mean," Bruce said, "when nobody's looking, you sit down with a pen and put words together and make a poem? What do you write about?"

"The same things you draw, I expect." The flush was dying away from his face, but his voice was still unsteady. He picked up a china cat and examined it minutely. "That's why—I expected you to know I wouldn't ever have teased you about drawing. I don't know why I expected you to know. Sometimes you expect people to read your mind. I thought perhaps your dad might have said something, but when I think about it, I know he wouldn't."

"Wait—What has Dad got to do with it?"

"He reads my poems."

"Dad?"

"Yes."

"He's never—he never said—"

"Of course not. I asked him not to tell anyone. I was afraid you'd laugh." The corners of his mouth went up. "That's why it's so funny . . . your dad's a good critic."

"I didn't even know he liked poetry. It's not—"

"Factual." He shrugged. "Perhaps he doesn't. But he reads mine, when I've got something I think is good. . . . I did an essay for one of his classes in a hurry. I wrote it on the back of one of my poems. He said the essay was terrible, but he liked the poem. So

I've been sneaking poems to him ever since. It's good to have someone else's opinion."

Bruce pushed the sides of the box flat. Above him, the study floor creaked; he glanced up as though he could see Uncle Harold through the floorboards. Then he looked at Alexander again, sitting big and loose-limbed among Mrs. Brewster's fragile glassware.

"Poetry. Can I—can I read some?"

"If you want." He looked toward the window. "I think they've stopped for the day. We'd better get the cardboard under the stone and clear out."

"Right."

The knuckles stood out white in Alexander's hands as he shifted the stone upward. Bruce slid the cardboard underneath it and it settled again, gently tilted.

"Let's put some boxes in front of it to hide it," Alexander said. "Oh. Your mother thinks we've gone fossil-hunting, in case she asks."

Bruce stared at him over a box of books. "Fossil-hunting? In Middleton? Why would she think that?"

"I don't know." He took a box from Carol's arms and added it to the stack in front of their work. "Perhaps it was something I said."

They drew the stone out the next morning after breaking through the rest of the mortar. They pulled the cardboard until the stone balanced delicately half-in, half-out of its place, and Bruce said, "Carol, move back in case we drop it."

She stepped back.

"Steady—" Alexander breathed. They shifted it, breaking the balance, their hands splayed beneath the cardboard. The unexpected weight of it broke through their hands. They jerked away. The stone hit the floor with a dull, ponderous thud and cracked.

Alexander closed his eyes. "How many toes have we got left among us?"

Bruce stared upward. There was no sound from the study. Carol uncurled her bare toes. She looked at the hole they had made, and something in the unbroken darkness behind it drew her forward. She stepped on the stone and pushed her arm through the hole.

"Bruce!"

"Half a minute—Here's the light—"

She drew back; he flicked it on over her shoulder. They were silent as the light melted through the darkness, traced an arch across it. Then Bruce's voice came, with a contentment she had never heard before in it, "Vaulted."

Alexander's breath whispered slow next to Carol's ear. An arch of stones ran before them into darkness over an earth floor.

"It's there," Carol whispered. "It's there. It was there all the time. It wasn't a legend. It was really there."

"I wonder if it still goes to the church."

"Shouldn't wonder," Alexander murmured. "I feel small inside. Humble. You've answered a riddle nobody else could answer. I wish we could squeeze through the hole. I say, Bruce—"

"What?"

He hesitated, staring into the tunnel. "When—Are you going to tell your Dad, now? He'll have to know, sometime."

"I know. So will Mrs. Brewster. I wish—"

"I wish it could be a secret," Carol said. Her voice was soft, muffled by the stone. "It's so quiet . . . like a piece of another world. And if we tell people, the first thing they'll say is—"

"However did you know?" Bruce said. "And then we'll get started on ghosts and Puritans and Madame Tussaud's waxworks, and Dad will tell us nicely but firmly that we didn't really see ghosts, which we did see. I think we found the tunnel, but we still haven't quite answered the riddle, and I'd rather keep it quiet until then."

"Which riddle?"

"Edward. Why the girl comes back at all. Why should she? What we should do is—"

"Open the tunnel," Carol said. "And the next time she says 'Come' we'll come."

Alexander smiled. "Follow a ghost. Right. I've always wanted to, but I never knew it." He drew another long slow breath. "Ghosts and a tunnel and a mystery. Such richness."

They worked straight through two more days. By the end of the third day there was a thin jagged hole in

Mrs. Brewster's cellar wall, almost big enough to squeeze through. They hid the hole, shoved the stones behind the table, and brushed themselves off, too weary even to speak. The house was empty when they went upstairs; Aunt Catherine and Uncle Harold had gone somewhere.

"Tomorrow," Bruce said. Alexander nodded, stifling a yawn. He went home. Carol went upstairs and washed the dust out of her hair. She brushed it dry beside her open window. Two long strips of the street next to the curbs were crumbled; they had begun to dig in one of them. The green truck was gone. She watched the sun slip behind the church spire, then behind the church. Then she saw Bruce come out with a wheelbarrow and hedge-clippers. He began to work slowly, letting the clippings fall heedlessly to the ground. He stopped once and looked down the long shaggy hedge that ran down the walk to the back of the house, where it curved upward into an arch that led to the side lawn. He yawned, scratching his head with the point of the clippers. Carol leaned back against the wall and watched him. The brush lay idle in her stiff aching hands. He blurred finally before her half-closed eyes, and she straightened, yawning, and began to brush again.

"What on earth have you been doing?" Aunt Catherine said at dinner. "You're both half-asleep in your plates."

Bruce blinked, stirring himself. "Oh. We—I've been

showing Carol a piece of Middleton. We were at it longer than we expected."

"What part did you see, Carol?"

She waved her hand vaguely. "That part across the field, where the farms are. I saw a bull. I've never seen one close before." She yawned in spite of herself.

Aunt Catherine looked at her, frowning a little. Then she said, "Well. A good night's rest will cure you. You've been so quiet, lately. I hope you're enjoying yourself."

"Oh, yes."

Uncle Harold cleared his throat. "I don't mean to nag," he said. "But there are dandelions all over the side lawn."

Bruce nodded. His hand lay lax around his milk glass, as though he were too tired to lift it. "I know. I'm sorry. I'll get to it. Tomor—Tomorrow."

Alexander did not come the next morning. They worked on two final stones that jutted into the hole and stopped their passage. Bruce called his house at noon.

"He's not there," he told Carol as they waited after lunch for the drilling to start again. "His mother sent him out to buy some new window-screens, and he came back and went again and she wanted to know where he was because he was supposed to put the screens in."

Carol wiggled her aching shoulders. "I wonder where he is."

"I hope he's here by four."

They moved the final stone at three-thirty. Bruce sat down on one of them and brushed at his face. His hands shook. He smiled at her, and the dust cracked on his face like a mask.

"I'm scared," she said. "What if—Bruce, what if we go through the tunnel and there's another century at the end of it. We'd be in the middle of a war."

"You can stay behind if you want. Then you can do all the explaining. What would you be—a Royalist or a Roundhead?"

"I don't know. I don't want to fight anybody. That's why I never liked history. Every time you turn a page in a history book, there's a different war going on."

"I know. But when—when two people can't even keep from fighting, it's hard to expect whole groups not to fight. But if that's all people did, they wouldn't be here still. They do other things. They build churches. Make wax statues. Write poetry, when nobody's looking. They build houses and tunnels that last for centuries. They do quiet things."

The drilling, quiet while he spoke, started up again with a spurt of noise.

"I wonder where Alexander is."

"Mm. Carol—"

"What?"

"Let's go in the tunnel now. Then, when she comes, if she speaks to us while we're there, we'll know that she's talking to us and not Edward."

"All right. You first."

He grinned, and disappeared halfway into the hole. The other half of him followed with a little maneuvering, and he vanished a moment. Then he rose and looked back at her, framed by stones. She giggled.

"You look like you're being walled in."

"Come on. Don't forget the light."

She wiggled in. The earth was hard and damp under her feet. The stones were damp. They curved in a flawless, unbroken arch above her head. She looked back and saw the cellar room, bright against the dark stones, oddly unfamiliar, as though she were seeing it for the first time.

"What time is it?"

He flashed the light at his watch. "Three-forty. You don't have to whisper."

"Neither do you."

The minutes dragged by in their silence. She stuck her fingers under her arms to warm them. Bruce's eyes glinted in the light as he looked around. Far, far away, somewhere beyond the jagged hole, the drilling sounded, stopped, sounded again.

"I wonder," Carol whispered, "if that's the way she sees the cellar. Or does she see it with somebody else's things in it, or just empty. . . ." A great black shape entered the hole as she looked, and the breath wailed from her. "Bruce—" The light danced as she caught his arm.

"Let go—" He steadied the light. A pair of golden

eyes flashed at him and he laughed. "That cat—Throw it back out—"

She reached for it, but it flattened itself beneath her hands and vanished into the shadows.

"Oh, well. Was it Emily's cat?"

"No. It was that black cat. . . ." Her mouth felt dry. "I think. . . . Bruce, turn around."

He turned. The man walked toward them down the tunnel, his footsteps soft, steady on the earth. The light winked off his sword. Bruce swallowed. He shifted aside; the man passed between them without a glance. They saw as he passed through the stones, the sunlight on the back of his black cape, on the broad brim of his hat. He stood just beyond the stones, listening, his head turning faintly in the direction of some sound.

He turned finally and came back through the stones, and as he passed them his stride quickened. Bruce held the light on him until he reached the edges of it and the shadows enveloped him. Even then they could hear the soft beat of his steps. Bruce turned back. The girl came toward them through the sunlight. They saw her face through the hole in the stones. She turned briefly before she entered, and they heard her voice.

"Edward. Come."

And suddenly they were no longer looking through a jagged hole, but through an arch of stone. A man, his head turned away from them as he looked back through the cellar, smiled briefly at her smile, and wax rolled down his fingers from the candle in his hand.

He was hidden in a dark cloak. It opened briefly as

he stepped through the arch, and they caught a glimpse of something silver that gleamed from a chain. He wore a plain hat that shadowed his face; it seemed young as he passed them, yet lean and set; he glanced back again, his eyes quick and watchful in the half-light. His hair beneath the hat was the same color as the girl's.

Carol's hands closed against her mouth. She felt tears gathering, stinging behind her eyes. Bruce touched her and she followed him, stumbling a little, blinking away the tears so she could see.

There was movement behind them. Bruce stopped abruptly, his breath hissing, and drew her flat beside him against the wall. A big man with a helm on his head passed them. He was armed at breast and back with steel plate; he carried a long spear with an ax blade wide and curved beneath it. Bruce's light swept over it and it flashed in a wedge of silver. Bruce made a small, inarticulate protest, as though he were asleep, protesting a dream. Another man followed the first, similarly dressed, with a sword unsheathed in his hand. They moved quickly ahead. Bruce followed them. Carol stared after him. She moved finally, running a little to catch up, and a sob welled in her throat and eased away and welled again.

There was a murmur of voices ahead in the darkness and then a sudden shout. There was a scream, a young girl's scream, high, light, endless. It grew louder and louder; Carol put her hands over her ears. A light flashed in her face, and she saw Bruce, turned back to her, saying something. She could not hear it above the scream. And then, as a stone dropped from the arch, thumped at her feet, the scream became the whine of the drilling above them. Another stone dropped. She saw Bruce's face, startled, turned upward. Then the stones broke and poured between them in a white shower of ancient mortar.

VIII

"Bruce!" The sound of her own voice startled
her, as though she had wakened herself, calling. The
mortar dust, thick, acrid, caught in her throat; she
coughed. She heard his coughing. The sound of it
twisted into a sharp dry sob and her heart stood still.
"Bruce!"

She stumbled over the stones. Light sprang at an
odd angle from the floor, near the wall. Above them,
the drilling continued in short strident bursts.

"Carol—"

"Where are you? Where are you? I can't see you—"
Her eyes flickered desperately over the shadowed
stones. Something shifted into the light; she went toward it, unsteady on the pile of stones.

"No—go back—" His voice broke again in the small
taut sound. Her fingers, icy, curled against her mouth.

"Go get Dad—Hurry—"

She ran down the dark tunnel, toward the small sunlit opening at the end of it. She climbed through and ran up the stairs to the quiet hall above, and as she slammed open the cellar door, three people turned toward her: Uncle Harold, opening the study door; Aunt Catherine at the open front door; and Alexander, whose face was suddenly shaken out of its calm. "Hurry—Uncle Harold, the tunnel fell in on Bruce —hurry—"

Uncle Harold came toward her. His face was strained, puzzled, as though he were trying to understand a language he did not know. He put his hands on her shoulders. "What? Carol, I want to help, but calm down and tell me—"

"The tunnel—the priest tunnel—" Her eyes moved past him to Alexander. "Tell them to stop drilling; it knocked the stones down on him—"

Uncle Harold's lips parted. "The priest tunnel? What—Carol, show me. You'll have to show me."

She led him and Aunt Catherine downstairs. Uncle Harold stopped at the sight of the hole, dark and jagged, in the wall, the stones neatly piled among Mrs. Brewster's books.

"You did this?" His voice was sharp with incredulity. Aunt Catherine followed Carol over to the hole. Carol turned, frightened at the tone of his voice.

"Yes."

"It *is* a tunnel," Aunt Catherine said wonderingly,

137

looking through over Carol's shoulder. She moved in after Carol; Uncle Harold followed them. The drilling had stopped; the tunnel was soundless, dark but for a tiny fan of light far ahead. Something blotted the light from the cellar; Alexander slipped through behind them.

"Where is he? I can't see—"

"Up there with the light."

The light shifted, pointed toward them as they came, and they stopped, blinking, at the edge of the fall of stones. "Bruce," Uncle Harold said. "Move the light downward if you can, so we can see what we're doing. Stay still."

"Dad, it was the drilling—"

"I know," Uncle Harold said. "Alexander stopped them." He reached Bruce and took the flashlight from him. Aunt Catherine knelt beside him. Uncle Harold shifted a stone; Bruce's breath hissed sharply.

"All right. Lie still. Catherine, call the hospital."

An ambulance came, and men maneuvered him through the hole and bore him away. Aunt Catherine and Uncle Harold followed in the car. The siren wailed down Parchment Street like a banshee, and Emily Raison came out, frightened and anxious, to find out what was wrong. Alexander explained. Carol stood, staring at the half-finished drains. The men had gone; the street lay torn and empty in the late afternoon. She wandered back into the yard. A breeze rustled through the half-cut hedge, stirred the dandelions. A lump burned dry in her throat; it would not go away.

"He's probably all right," Alexander said. "There weren't any stones on his head or his back. He was still talking."

"They wouldn't let him walk out."

"They never do until they know what's wrong."

Carol sat down on the front step. Her head dropped onto her knees; she closed her eyes and saw again the darkness of the tunnel. "Where were you, anyway? Why didn't you come?"

He dropped beside her, sighing. "Oh. I had a long conversation with Mrs. Brewster about flowers."

"Flowers?"

"Squashed flowers. The kind you get when five bicycles ride over them in your front lawn. She got it into her head that I had something personal against her flowers, just because I happened to be riding a bicycle. When she finally let me go, I rode to Sandy's house and had a long conversation with him about flowers. I'm ten times bigger than he is, and he was nervous, but he'll probably do something malicious, because he didn't like being lectured by me. But I was angry. And then I remembered what time it was. Did you follow the girl?"

Carol nodded. She sat hunched over herself, holding her arms, and her throat tightened, hurting. She swallowed. "She came, and she said 'Edward. Come,' and he came."

"Edward came?"

"Yes. He had a hat and a long cloak on, and he was carrying a candle. His hair was the same color as hers." She swallowed again. Tears formed, hot and swollen, behind her eyes. "And we followed them. And people followed us—men with swords and helmets—and they walked past us and they didn't see us. So, the Puritan had gone in before Edward, and he was waiting in the tunnel in front of him, and the men came in after him, and they all had swords and I think—I think—The tunnel fell in before we could see anything, but just before it fell, I could hear her screaming."

The wind rose, shivered through the leaves above the wall. Alexander stirred, drawing breath.

"They're all dead, you know. It happened centuries ago. There's no need to feel sad."

"That's the funny part. Bruce was trying to tell me about the light, but I didn't think it was important, until today. When he—when the men in armor went by, and when Bruce pointed the flashlight at them, the light reflected off the armor as if—as if they were real in our century . . . or we were real in theirs."

"I wish I'd been there. Oh, I wish I'd been there. Life is so unfair. Were you frightened?"

A tear ran down her bent face. "Only—only for Edward. She was leading him through, and he must have been her brother or a cousin, and I think they killed him right in front of her, and she can't—it's like when something terrible happens and you can't sleep—"

"Are you crying?" he said anxiously.

She rubbed her face with her sleeve. "No. But I don't see why everything had to go wrong at once. I don't see why they had to kill Edward—What difference does it make if you wear lace collars or plain collars, or if you like stained glass windows or plain windows, or if you like running around barefoot or drawing cows—There's enough room for all those things, isn't there?"

"Sometimes not," Alexander said. "There's not enough room in people's heads." He stood up. "I've got to call my mother and tell her why I'm not at home putting up screens. I'll stay here and wait for your aunt and uncle with you, because they've probably started wondering by now how we found the tunnel, and when you start explaining about the ghosts, you'll need someone of sane and sober character to back you up."

Carol straightened. "I forgot about that." She sighed, brushing mortar dust out of her hair. "I thought we were already past the hard part."

Alexander called his mother, and then they sat in the living room watching for Uncle Harold and Aunt Catherine out of the window. They came home finally, late in the evening. Carol opened the front door for them, and Aunt Catherine's tired face eased into a smile.

"Carol, you're still as white as a ghost. What is that all over you?"

"Centuries-old mortar, I should think," Uncle Harold said. "Bruce instructed me that I was not to plague you for explanations; he is going to explain everything when he comes home, but I doubt if I can wait that long."

"What—what's the matter with him?"

"Nothing too serious—cracked ribs and a twisted ankle and a large assortment of bruises. They're keeping him overnight, but he'll probably be home tomorrow." He paused a moment, looking at her. He rubbed his eyes wearily. "You could both have so easily been seriously hurt. . . . Why in heaven's name didn't Bruce tell me what you were doing? Or you, Alexander? You have some sense. I think it's a marvelous thing to have found; I want to know how you found it, but I wish you had not been so secretive. A man has a right to know when people are digging tunnels directly beneath him."

"Come into the kitchen," Aunt Catherine said. I'll fix you some supper. Alexander, does your mother know where you are?"

"Yes," Alexander said. His face was flushed slightly. He looked at Uncle Harold. "Sometimes, there are words that are hard to say."

"What is so difficult about saying you have discovered a tunnel?"

"That's easy to say. Most people go through life not knowing what a priest tunnel is. It's natural. They don't need one. But a priest tunnel is the sort of thing that you can show to people and they'll say 'I never

142

knew they existed, but now I'm seeing one, so they must exist.' But other things aren't so easy."

"Alexander," Uncle Harold said. "The easiest thing to do would be just to say it."

"No, it wouldn't," Carol said. "Uncle Harold, do you remember the ghost I saw in the cellar?"

"Ghost—oh. Yes."

"Well, it was a ghost."

Uncle Harold opened his mouth to say something. Then he stopped and closed it. Aunt Catherine stared at Carol. She blinked and gave her head a little shake, as though she were waking herself up.

"I think," she said, "we should all sit down and talk."

They sat at the kitchen table. Uncle Harold lit his pipe, looking at them between puffs of smoke. Aunt Catherine peeled potatoes at the sink behind them as she listened.

"There are no such things as ghosts," Uncle Harold said.

"There," Alexander said. "You see? Ghosts are like priest tunnels—you don't expect them to exist until you see them."

"But what have ghosts got to do with the priest tunnel?"

"They walked through it," Carol said. "That's how we knew it was there."

Uncle Harold was silent. The rhythmic scrape of the potato-peeler was the only sound in the kitchen. Carol felt the blood welling to her face beneath the mortar dust. Alexander was still beside her, watching Uncle Harold. He said finally, "They weren't green and hairy."

"What?" Uncle Harold said, startled.

"The ghosts. One of them was the girl in the painting in your study. That's the arch, you know, behind her—the priest tunnel. The other one wasn't so nice. He nearly walked through me with a sword."

"He was a Puritan," Carol said. "Like the one in Madame Tussaud's statues of 'When Did You Last See Your Father?' "

"Wait," Uncle Harold said. "You saw a ghost in the cellar who looked like a Puritan in Madame Tussaud's museum, and you assumed that where he walked through the wall, the priest tunnel was there?"

"People usually don't walk through walls for no reason," Carol said.

"I know, but what made you decide specifically a priest tunnel was there?"

"Bruce said there was," Alexander said. "I've always wanted a tunnel. To go through, you know. That's what the girl was doing—going in the tunnel."

"She would come," Carol said, "and she'd say 'Edward. Come.' Only we never saw Edward, and that confused us, because we could see the Puritan who was waiting to kill Edward, and—"

"Wait," Uncle Harold said again. Aunt Catherine had turned.

"How did you know the Puritan wanted to kill Edward?" she asked curiously. Uncle Harold looked at her helplessly.

"We didn't," Carol said, "until today. Then we got the tunnel open and we went in, and when the girl said, 'Edward. Come,' he came. The Puritan was waiting for him ahead, and we followed Edward and the girl, and then soldiers started coming from behind us, and then the girl screamed ahead of us in the darkness —and the tunnel fell in on Bruce."

Uncle Harold gazed at her, his pipe motionless in one hand. "You've been seeing ghosts in this house all the while you've been here? Why didn't you tell Catherine or me?"

"I tried. And Bruce tried." Her voice stuck; she paused, clearing her throat. "He said—he said one day he took you down to the cellar to see one, and you couldn't see it. And we—we told Father Malory, because priests are interested in dead people, and he came to see them and—he couldn't."

"Oh." Uncle Harold leaned back in his chair, his face easing.

"But I saw them," Alexander said.

"You did. Why couldn't I see them?"

"I think," Carol said, "that if she had to watch those men kill Edward, she probably didn't want to see anyone old enough to do that again."

Aunt Catherine turned back to the sink. "That seems reasonable."

145

"Catherine," Uncle Harold said. "There are no such things as ghosts."

"So my niece with my red hair is barmy. And so is your son. Or are you suggesting they bothered to do such a childish thing as to invent a tale like this? I would rather believe in ghosts."

"But it's incredible."

Alexander looked at Carol. "That means it's unbelievable. I wouldn't invent anything so unbelievable. People invent things to have them believed. Incredible things just happen on their own."

"I didn't want it to happen," Carol said. "I didn't want to see ghosts in your cellar."

Uncle Harold sighed. "Tell me about it from the beginning."

He was silent while she told him what had happened since she had first seen the ghosts. Aunt Catherine made their supper quietly, a frown between her brows as she listened. When Carol was finished, Uncle Harold sat for a long time without speaking. Aunt Catherine set a plate of food in front of him, and he said finally, "There must be some logical explanation."

"There isn't," Alexander said. "I tried to think up one, but I couldn't."

"Was there a crack in the stones or a change of coloring in the mortar that outlined the priest tunnel?"

"I didn't see one," Carol said. "Emily Raison said Mrs. Brewster looked for the tunnel and she couldn't find it."

146

"Do you want some supper, Alexander?" Aunt Catherine said.

"Yes, please."

She filled a plate for him. "I think the whole thing sounds very logical."

"Perhaps, but. . . ." Uncle Harold's voice trailed away. He stared down at his teacup.

Alexander said mildly, "We aren't trying to play a trick on you. None of us would do that. Not even me."

"All right. I'm sorry, but it had occurred to me. You and Bruce are occasionally unscrupulous."

Alexander blushed. "I know," he said. "But we aren't trying to hide anything from you. We could have said the mortar was a different color where they filled the tunnel opening. That's much easier to say than that we saw ghosts walking through walls."

"I think," Aunt Catherine said, sitting down, "it's a shame that on Carol's first visit here she has to be troubled by ghosts."

"It disturbs me," Uncle Harold said, "that neither Father Malory nor I could see them. Has anyone else you know seen them?"

"No."

Uncle Harold sighed. He unfolded his napkin. "Well. Perhaps someone has been playing an elaborate trick on you. But it did result in a tunnel, and you must have had a few rough days opening that. I'll talk to Bruce about it tomorrow; perhaps he can shed some light on the mystery."

"Somebody," Aunt Catherine said, "has to tell Mrs. Brewster she now owns a cellar with a hole and a tunnel in it."

"Oh, lord," said Uncle Harold. "I suppose I must."

He brought Bruce home the next morning. Carol watched him hobble down the walk with a crutch under one arm. His face was pulled into a scowl to hide the pain that twitched at it occasionally. Uncle Harold walked slowly beside him, wincing at every shift of the crutch. Aunt Catherine met them at the door.

"There's a nice fresh bed ready for you," she said. "I'll bring you some aspirin when you lie down; that'll ease the pain."

"I don't want to stay in bed for a whole week," Bruce said. He sounded close to tears.

Aunt Catherine said grimly, "You're lucky you don't have to stay in bed the rest of your life." She felt his flushed face. "And I don't want to see you downstairs until you can walk down on your own two feet."

"What did Mrs. Brewster say about the tunnel?"

"She hasn't, yet," Uncle Harold said. Bruce glanced at him doubtfully. He looked at Carol, and she said, "We told him."

"Oh." His breath gathered and loosed in a long, slow sigh. He went to the stairs and began his slow, halting progress up them. Uncle Harold went to his side.

"Let me carry your crutch," he said gently. "I don't

148

know where to touch you without hurting you, but perhaps if you lean on me it won't be so difficult."

Bruce gave him the crutch. He put his arm around Uncle Harold's shoulders. Aunt Catherine stood at the foot of the stairs and watched them until they disappeared around the bend in the stairs and Bruce's door clicked open. Then she stirred herself. She looked at Carol.

"He'll be cross for the next few days. If he snarls at you, snarl back."

Carol smiled. The movement of her face felt strange, as though she had not smiled for a long time. Aunt Catherine's arm dropped lightly across her shoulders.

Carol said slowly, "Do you believe us? About the ghosts?"

She was silent a moment, her brows tugging together. "Yes," she said finally. "This house is very old, and I think that must be only one of the strange sad things that may have happened in it. I don't know anything about ghosts, but I hope that somehow opening the tunnel will put the girl's mind at rest, because three hundred years is too long a time to spend haunting a cellar. I wouldn't want to do it."

"Bruce says ghosts might be only reflections of people living."

"Perhaps."

"But I don't think that's what we saw yesterday. It was more than a reflection, and I think she knew we were there." She shivered suddenly, and Aunt Catherine's hold tightened.

"I think she chose the right people to appear to. Under the circumstances, you behaved very sensibly, in your own fashion, and I hope Mrs. Brewster appreciates that."

"I suppose she'll ask how we found it."

"I think she might enjoy having ghosts in her cellar. After all, she does like old things."

"I suspect she might draw the line at three-hundred-year-old people," Uncle Harold said, coming back down the stairs. "Bruce is in bed. I think he's feverish. They prescribed some medicine that will help him sleep." He took a bottle out of his sweater pocket and gave it to her. "I'll call Mrs. Brewster now."

He went to the kitchen. Aunt Catherine went upstairs with Bruce's medicine. Carol sat down on the bottom step and watched the huge pendulum in the grandfather clock trace its silent path back and forth, back and forth. The closed door and the thick stones of the house muffled the drilling. The hall was cool and changeless. She wondered for a moment what the house had looked like out of the blue eyes of a young girl three centuries before, as she came down the stairs in her long dress with its lace collar. The stairs creaked behind her and she jumped. Aunt Catherine came down.

"He's asleep," she said softly, as if the sound of her voice might wake him. The kitchen door opened, and they turned. Uncle Harold came out. His mouth was crooked; he ran his fingers through his hair and sighed.

"Some people," he said, "have no historical perspective."

"She didn't like it," Aunt Catherine said. He shook his head.

"She wants it closed."

Carol stared at him. Her breath caught in a gasp. "She can't—she can't close it up—she can't—not after all that work! It's not right! We spent hours opening it, and my hands are all blistered, and it's our tunnel, and if she closes it the girl will keep coming back for another three hundred years, and where else is she going to find people who won't get hysterical and run like Susan did—" She began to sob helplessly. Uncle Harold drew her against him; she felt the soft wool of his sweater, smelling of pipe-smoke, against her face.

"We won't give up that easily," he said soothingly.

"Bruce—Bruce couldn't take it being closed up—he couldn't—He'd run away, or something."

Uncle Harold found a handkerchief in his pocket and gave it to her. "I hope not," he said. She straightened, wiping her face, her breath catching in quick jerks. "Carol, when I called Mrs. Brewster, she was upset at something the boys had done to her garden, and that's why—"

"Bruce didn't do it; neither did Alexander. He told me about it. Sandy squashed her flowers."

"I know, but Bruce has been in trouble with her before, and if he's reformed, she hasn't found out yet. She was in no mood to appreciate anything any of the boys had done. She was too upset with them to understand properly that she has the only priest tunnel in England. If she begins to understand that, she might change her mind."

"Perhaps if she sees it, she'll change her mind," Aunt Catherine said. Uncle Harold sighed.

"The problem will be to get her down here. I think

she expects me to wall it up personally. I can't do that; it goes against all my principles."

"What are you going to do, then?" Carol said.

"The only thing I can do. Procrastinate."

Carol went up to see Bruce in the afternoon. She opened his door quietly, peeked in, and found him awake, looking at her.

"Oh, it's you," he said. His brows were drawn in a dark line. He waved at the chair beside his bed. "Sit down. I'm sorry you had to do all the explaining."

"Alexander helped." She moved a water glass and the medicine off the chair and sat down. Bruce picked at threads in his cover.

"Did he believe you?"

"He believed us. I'm not sure if he believed the ghosts."

"How can he believe us and not believe in them? He must think we're either barmy or lying. Did he call Mrs. Brewster?"

"Yes."

"What did she say?"

She hesitated. He watched her, his eyes steady under his frown, and she said finally, "She's not sure."

"Not sure? Is she coming to see it? She is, isn't she?"

She shook her head, her throat burning again. Bruce stared at her; he shifted impatiently, trying to sit up.

"Carol, what did she say?"

"She said—she—Bruce, why did you have to bother

her so much! We did all that work for nothing, and all because you probably rode circles around her one day, and now you could draw the most beautiful picture in the world and she still wouldn't like it because you did it—"

Bruce dropped back on the pillows. "She wants it closed," he said levelly. His eyes were black in his white face.

"Yes, because Sandy ruined her flowers, and she thinks you and Alexander did it because you're always doing things—"

"I suppose you've never done anything wrong in your life—"

"Of course I have! And I'm wishing now that I'd never done anything, ever, that hurt anybody, because it just ends in people being killed, or hurt inside so much that they don't trust people, or they can't think straight enough to even like priest tunnels that other people dig up for them."

Bruce sighed. He dropped a hand over his eyes. "Oh, well," he said, and the weariness of his voice startled her.

"Oh well what?"

"I don't know. I don't know what to do. I can't think. My thoughts won't lie still. There's nothing we can do."

"There must be."

"It's her cellar, her priest tunnel."

"We opened it. Bruce, that girl might have to haunt

the cellar for another three hundred years if we close it now."

"She might just do it anyway." He stirred restlessly. "I don't want to think about it. Carol, go away, or stop lecturing me, or something. I can't think now. I'll think tomorrow."

She stood up. Then she looked down at him, seeing his heavy eyes and the taut pull of his mouth, and her clenched hands opened. "I'm sorry," she said softly. "I forgot what it's like to be sick. I'm not sick very often. The last time I had to stay in bed, it was because I fell off a skate-board into a brick geranium planter and broke my ankle. I hated it. It wasn't funny."

"It sounds like something that could only happen to you. I'll think of a way out. I promise. But everything happened so fast, it's all jumbled in my head. And I didn't even get the hedges cut. You'd think I could do something right for a change, now that I'd like to."

The door opened softly. Aunt Catherine came in. She went to Bruce and felt his forehead. "Are you hungry?"

"No. I'm thirsty, though. Are there any lemons?"

"I'll get some. You try and sleep."

Carol followed her out. She paused at the foot of the stairs, thinking. "I think I used my last lemons in a pie. Would you go over and see if Emily has some to lend me?"

Emily Raison opened her front door even before Carol opened the gate. Her face was wrinkled with anxiety. "Oh, my dear, is he all right? Does Catherine need something? Come in a moment and sit down; you've been running. What is it, then?"

Carol stepped into her neat parlor. She sank into a fat chair, catching her breath. "Aunt Catherine wants to know if she can borrow some lemons, because Bruce wants some lemonade. He's all right. He's sick, but he'll live."

"Oh, I'm so glad. You sit there, and I'll find some. I'll be back directly." She disappeared into her kitchen. Carol rose, prowling restlessly around the room, picking up china what-nots and putting them down again. Geraldine the cat lifted her head from the depths of a chair and yawned. The room was silent, full of old things without a speck of dust on them, each with its own particular spot. There were doilies on the armchairs and glass flowers and candlesticks on a tiny table and dark, framed photographs on the walls and on the mantel. She looked at the stern faces, wondering if they had ever smiled. She turned, and something above the piano caught her eye. She went toward it, not breathing, and knelt on the piano bench, staring at it where it hung in its own place on the wall.

"There," Emily Raison said. "I didn't use them after all. Here you are, my dear. Tell your aunt—"

"Who did that?"

"What?" She looked at the wall. "Oh, the needlework? Mrs. Brewster did that when she was a little girl. She copied it from the painting in the study."

"I know, but why did she—" She stopped abruptly, shaking her head. The girl looked down at her, blurred a little by uneven stitching, and behind her was not a dark arch but a smooth wall of unbroken grey stone. Carol felt something in her throat too wide to swallow. "I wonder . . ." she whispered. "I wonder. . . ."

"Yes, it is nice, isn't it? She gave it to me as a memento when I left service. She was very good with a needle when she was small. Here are the lemons."

Carol took them. "Thank you," she said. "Thank you, Emily Raison."

IX

BRUCE WAS ASLEEP WHEN SHE GOT BACK. HE SLEPT fitfully through the night. She woke once at his sudden shout and struggled out of bed to stand blinking in the hall light until Aunt Catherine came out of his bedroom.

"He said he was dreaming about the hedges," she said, puzzled. Carol yawned.

"He didn't get them cut."

"But it doesn't matter," Aunt Catherine said. She shook her head and went back to bed. He did not wake again until lunchtime, and then they heard his voice, faint down the stairs, demanding food.

Carol took him a tray. He maneuvered carefully to a sitting position, and she put it on his knees. He looked down at it.

"What's that?"

"Poached egg on toast."

"I'm supposed to eat it?"

"No. You can throw it out the window if you want."

He poked at it doubtfully with his fork. Carol drew the curtains and sat down on the window-seat. The light splashed across the bed; his face was pale in it, but the shadows beneath his eyes were gone.

"I'm glad you weren't hurt," he said. "You could have been hurt so easily, if you had been close behind me."

"I might have gotten killed," she said thoughtfully. "Then I could have haunted the cellar, too."

"That's not funny."

"Well, I didn't, so there's no use thinking about it, is there?"

He was silent a moment, looking at the egg. "I suppose not. But it frightened me. Perhaps I should start thinking before I do things, instead of jumping into them, like I jumped into the blackberry bushes. But then, that was probably the most stupid thing I'll ever do."

He took a bite of egg. Carol leaned back against the windowsill. She smelled sun-warmed grass on the warm air. The drilling had stopped for the weekend; the afternoon was soundless. "I wonder where the tunnel ends. I wonder if there still is an ending to it, a place where you can come out."

"Maybe Dad can talk to Mrs. Brewster so we can find out. He's good at talking to people."

"He doesn't want it closed. He said he was going to procrastinate."

Bruce stirred restlessly. "I can't understand why she's not even curious. She likes old things. She loves this old house, and all the antiques in it. Why doesn't she want a three-hundred-year-old tunnel in her cellar? That's an antique."

"She's angry."

"I know, but. . . . She's not thinking logically. I wish she would. I was tempted, before you came up, to try to sneak downstairs and go through the tunnel, but it takes me five minutes even to sit up. . . . Have you gone through?" he asked a little wistfully, and she shook her head.

"I won't go without you. Anyway, I'm not going now—not so soon after you got hurt. It scared me, too."

"I dreamed about it falling last night. . . . The hedge was growing in it, and it pushed at the top of the tunnel, and knocked the stones loose." He finished half a glass of lemonade, then asked, "Where was Alexander? Why wasn't he there when we went through?"

She told him. He was silent when she finished, tracing a delicate design on his napkin with the point of his knife. He put it down finally and shifted the tray off his knees to the bed. "I suppose it's no use telling her we were tearing open her cellar wall when someone ran over her flowers. It doesn't matter really. It may as well have been me. I would have, I think, except that I like flowers. But I've done other things. . . . But it still doesn't seem right that we've done all that work for nothing. There must be something we can do." He was silent again, looking at her as she sat on the window-seat. He said suddenly, "Turn your head a little, away from the light. Can I draw it?"

"What for?"

"Because there are some lines in it that make me want to draw it. I don't have anything else to do. Do you mind sitting still?"

She shook her head. "Nobody ever drew me before. Can I talk? What lines do you want to draw? I don't have wrinkles, do I?"

He smiled. "No. Would you get my things out of the window-seat? The tablet and the pencil-case. . . . Thanks. Put your hair back and look at the light-shade. No. Look at the dresser top. Don't smile."

"I can't help it."

"All right. Smile."

The door squeaked open half an hour later, and Alexander stuck his head into the room. "Hello," he said gently. "I came to visit the sick. I brought you a flower, and I thought I would read you some soothing poetry." He put a purple thistle in Bruce's water glass and looked at the drawing. "I say, who's that beautiful girl?"

Bruce smiled down at it contentedly. "It's in the bone structure. You miss it when she's got her hair all over her face."

Carol's feet hit the floor with a thump. "Let me see."

"I'm not finished—"

"I'm getting a crick in my neck." She leaned across the bed to look at it. Bruce glanced up at her sudden silence.

"Don't you like it? I'm not quite finished."

She stared down at the still face, fine-boned and delicately shaded, oddly unfamiliar. "That's not me."

"I tried to make it like you. Sit down again; I'm still shading. You're not used to seeing your face on flat paper."

"I think it is like you," Alexander said.

"But where's the rest of my hair?"

"Tied back."

She sat down slowly. Alexander sat down on the chair. "I never called you a matchstick. I have a great respect for bones, living and dead. Speaking of dead bones, I don't think it's fair that you had all that adventure without me. I worked just as hard to open the tunnel."

Bruce's pencil checked. "I know. We waited as long as we could for you." He paused briefly. "There's a problem."

"Another one? Bring on your problem. After telling your dad we've been seeing ghosts, we can tackle anything. What is it?"

"Mrs. Brewster. She wants the tunnel closed."

Alexander's mouth moved in a silent whistle. It settled into a thin line. He bent down to pick up the water glass and sat a moment looking at the thistle. "I can guess," he said softly. "She was that angry when she talked to me. But I never thought her reason was impaired. Doesn't she like ghosts?"

"I don't know."

Carol looked away from the dresser. "Bruce—"

"I don't know what to do." He leaned back, tired, his hands still.

"She'll like it when she sees it," Alexander said. "Perhaps we should kidnap her and leave her in the middle of it. Perhaps you should do something nice to her, and she'll have to come and thank you. Be charming."

"I don't know how."

"Bruce," Carol said again. "Miss Emily has something on her wall—" There were footsteps outside of Bruce's door, and she stopped. Uncle Harold opened the door. Father Malory followed him in.

"Hello," Father Malory said. "I didn't mean to interrupt anything, but I wanted to hear about the ghosts. Do you mind telling me?"

Bruce shook his head. "I don't mind." He looked past him to Uncle Harold, shaking the ashes out of his pipe. "You haven't said anything. I can't tell if you believe us or not."

Uncle Harold was silent a moment. "Does it matter what I think?"

"Yes."

"Then I can only say that I haven't enough evidence to form a conclusion one way or the other. You'll have to be satisfied with that, Bruce."

"You don't believe us."

"I didn't say—"

"We aren't lying."

"I know."

Bruce moved impatiently under the bedclothes, his brows drawn. "Well, you must think something. I just don't want you to think we're lying or we're crazy, and if you don't believe us, what else can you think?"

Uncle Harold sighed. "I don't think the matter is so important that I must form a conclusion from it on either your sanity or your principles." He reached behind Alexander to drop the ashes in the wastebasket. "People inevitably see things differently. The important thing is that we don't have to quarrel about who is right or—"

He stopped. He stood quietly, the pipe motionless in his hand, looking down at the picture beneath Bruce's hands. His eyes moved from it, incredulous, to Bruce's face. Bruce swallowed. He shifted, trying to sit straight. Uncle Harold dropped the pipe in his pocket, clearing his throat.

"That's nice. Quite nice. It's amazing, isn't it, how little you can know about a person even after fourteen years." He turned to go. Bruce leaned forward, his breath catching with the effort, and gripped his arm.

"Dad—" Uncle Harold looked down at him wordlessly. Bruce was silent a moment, his mouth tight, his hand tight on Uncle Harold's wrist. He said steadily, "We were having a sort of an argument. Carol says it doesn't look like her, because it's too beautiful, and Alexander says it does. I think Carol is just too used to thinking she's skinny and ugly to see herself properly even when she looks in a mirror, perhaps because she's been teased too much. But I was trying to draw what I saw. What do you think?"

"I think—" He stopped, and cleared his throat. "I think you have an incredible eye for fact."

"I knew I was right," Alexander said complacently. Bruce let go of Uncle Harold. He held out the tablet.

"You can look through it if you want. Most of my good ones are in there, except for some flowers that Alexander has. That's how I got that black eye."

Uncle Harold looked up a little dazedly from the tablet. "Drawing flowers?"

"And cows. That one is the cow." He watched the smile break slowly across Uncle Harold's face. He lay back again, watching him. Father Malory looked over his shoulder as he turned pages. He said after a moment, "I saw you do that one, during mass. I'm sure that was one of my more garbled sermons."

Bruce glanced at him surprisedly. "I didn't think you saw me. I wanted to do your face in front of the rose window, with the light coming in."

"What's this one?" Uncle Harold said. "It looks like a seventeenth century—" His voice faded. He stared at Bruce, startled.

"Oh, that's the ghost," Alexander said cheerfully. "He nearly walked through me, but I moved. Now I wish I hadn't. How many chances do you get in life to let a ghost walk through you? I might have enjoyed it."

Uncle Harold closed his eyes. He held them closed a moment with his fingers. "Ghosts," he said. "Priest tunnels. Bruce McQueen da Vinci Lawrence, my son.

It's too much for one man to bear in the short space of two days. I need a long vacation." He dropped his hand. "Or have you completely finished startling me?"

"I can't think of anything else," Bruce said. "Did you see the one of Emily Raison? I climbed up her apple tree to get that. She was washing graves."

Father Malory chuckled. "Yes. I like that one."

"She told us about the priest tunnel," Carol said. "She believed in it when no one else did."

"Did she? Perhaps I should go through it, in case we have another Civil War."

"It's too dangerous now," Uncle Harold said. "Look at this one—sheep blocking the road to Chelveston."

"Mrs. Brewster might seal it up while you're still in there," Alexander said. Father Malory raised his eyes.

"Are you joking?"

"Only a little. I'm sure she wouldn't do it on purpose."

"But she does want to? Why?"

"We annoyed her," Bruce said.

"Why?"

He flushed slightly. "It seemed like a good idea at the time."

"Sow the wind and reap the whirlwind," Father Malory murmured. "Harold, can't you talk to her?"

"He's my son. I'm responsible for his disreputable character."

"You are not," Bruce said. "I'm old enough to do

some things by myself."

Uncle Harold smiled. He closed the tablet. "There's no arguing that. Do you mind—do you mind if I take this with me and look through it more carefully? I'm sure your mother would like to see it. Or has she?"

Bruce shook his head. "No one has but you and Carol." He stifled a yawn. His eyelids curved like half-moons. Uncle Harold reached across him to pick up the tray.

"You're tired. We'll go and let you rest."

"Father Malory wanted to hear about the ghosts."

"I'll tell him," Carol said, getting up. "You didn't eat your lunch. Aunt Catherine said I was supposed to make you eat all of it. But I don't feel like nagging. You're old enough to know better."

Bruce laughed. "Come back and nag me about supper. Dad—"

Uncle Harold turned at the doorway. "What?"

"You keep a good secret, too."

"I do?"

Alexander dropped his face in his hands. "He guessed my fatal secret."

"Oh." Uncle Harold laughed. "I was wondering how long I might have to keep that."

Father Malory looked at Alexander as he moved, big-boned and placid, toward the door. "Do you draw, too?"

"No. I write poetry."

Father Malory blinked. He smiled contentedly.

"How marvelous."

He listened quietly, sitting in the living room, while Carol told him what happened when they went through the tunnel. When she finished he said, "You didn't actually see Edward killed?"

"No. They were too far ahead of us."

"Perhaps he was only captured," Uncle Harold said absently, looking through Bruce's tablet. Father Malory smiled.

"Perhaps. . . . What was he wearing?"

"I couldn't see anything besides his long cloak and his hat. He was dressed in black, maybe because he was hiding."

"It wouldn't be that much protection at four o'clock in the afternoon," Uncle Harold murmured. "Black was a popular color in those days."

Father Malory glanced down at his black suit. "Perhaps he was a priest, then, rather than a Royalist leader." He was silent a moment, his eyes on the quiet afternoon. "There was a great deal of religious intolerance, then, on all sides. The strong Anglican church persecuted the Catholics, the Puritans, the Quakers, and the smaller groups of people who had their own particular beliefs. And the Puritans, as they gained power, persecuted the Anglican church, since that was the state religion, and they tore apart churches and sent priests into flight. It's much more peaceful these days. People have their own faiths; they argue just as much, but they rarely fight about them."

169

Uncle Harold looked up. "Speaking of arguments, how did the boys play this morning?"

"Oh, they did nicely. Roger Simmons broke down in the middle of his cello solo from shyness, but other than that. . . ." He sighed. "None of the older people liked it, except the boys' parents."

"Why not?" Carol said.

"People aren't used to modern music in medieval churches. Old Mrs. Crane said she was going to complain to the Bishop, but the Bishop is used to me. The boys were so disappointed. Roger Simmons cried."

"Does that mean they can't play anymore?"

"I don't know. I haven't decided what to do yet. The young people like it, but I don't want to divide the parish on an issue like that."

"Argument is inevitable."

"I know, but I wish I could find a way of pleasing everybody. So much time is wasted arguing about things instead of enjoying them."

Carol nodded. "Like Mrs. Brewster and the priest tunnel. She'd enjoy it if she saw it, but she won't come."

"She called me about it this morning," Uncle Harold said. "I tried to persuade her to come, and she said she had no interest in seeing anything my son had done. She doesn't want all the boys in the neighborhood running through it, bothering priests and breaking her antiques and getting flattened by falling rocks. I have a feeling I could find her at any moment on the doorstep with a bag of cement and a trowel."

"What are you going to do, then?" Father Malory asked.

"I don't know," he said wearily. "If I don't close it, she'll send someone to have it done, and if I do close it I will never be able to look at my niece, or my son, or my face in the mirror again. It is dangerous; she's quite right about that, but I think it can be fixed, if only they would stop that drilling over it."

"You haven't gone through it, then."

"No. I have been sorely tempted, but Catherine won't let me. She says if I got hit by a falling rock I would deserve it for going through when I expect Carol and Alexander to stay out of it. I suppose she's right. Some of those stones are huge, and I heard one drop in the night when I went down to look in. . . . I wonder if perhaps it was built earlier than the Civil War, perhaps during the religious persecutions of the Tudor monarchs when the church across the road was forced to turn Protestant, and Catholics worshipped secretly. . . . This house would have been different, then; I'm not sure it would have had a cellar. But perhaps the people living in it were dedicated enough to build a tunnel, shelter priests. . . ." He reached forward to touch the grey, uneven stones of the fireplace, his eyes vague with thought. "The house would have been a single story, built on these great flagstones, with the hearth running the length of it, and that strong beam supporting the ceiling. . . . In spring they

171

would have put fresh flowers on the stone floor and rushes against the chill . . . and perhaps one spring, when the earth had thawed after the winter snow, and people were arguing and fighting and dying over the changes that had come, they began to build a tunnel for priests and people who would not change. . . ." His hand dropped. "Well. There's no way of knowing for sure."

The church bells rang a quarter-hour across the stillness. "I wonder where it ends," Father Malory said dreamily. He looked down at his watch and rose. "I must go. No—don't bother to see me out." He opened the door before Uncle Harold could rise. "I should go and see Mrs. Murphy about her arthritis; she gets very lonely, especially on a quiet Sunday." He closed the door. They heard the front door open and close. Uncle Harold turned a final page in Bruce's tablet.

"My son," he murmured. "Fighting for the sake of Art." He stood up. "I'd better show this to his mother."

The drilling began again the next morning. Carol heard it as she went upstairs with a breakfast tray. She thumped it crossly on Bruce's knees and orange juice spilled into his egg.

"Hey!" he said sleepily. She righted the glass, flushing.

"I'm sorry. I was listening to the drilling. I'll get you

another egg; I drowned this one."

"I don't want another egg. That's all right. I'll eat the toast and jam and the chocolate and the bacon."

"Mrs. Brewster called again." She sat down on the window-seat, drawing her knees up, and frowned at the workmen digging in the street. Bruce stirred; his tray rattled again.

"I wish she would stop annoying Dad. I'm going to get up today, and I'm going through that tunnel at four o'clock, and I don't care what anybody says afterward."

Carol eyed him coldly. "How are you going to get your crutch through the hole?"

"I'll manage. You can come and help."

"I will not. I already saw the tunnel fall on you once, and that's enough."

"Then I'll go by myself."

"Go ahead. Jumping in the blackberries was stupid enough, but at least you didn't go back and do it again."

"Then what are we going to do?" he demanded. "Sit quietly and let Mrs. Brewster close it? How are we ever going to know what happened to Edward if we don't follow the girl all the way through? That's what we opened the tunnel for, isn't it? This might be the last day we've got before she closes it—we've got to try, at least—"

"All right! I'll get Alexander to go with me."

"I'm coming, too."

"Bruce, you couldn't keep up with us. You would just be in the way of all the ghosts—they'd walk right through you. And if the tunnel fell in on you again, I wouldn't want to be around to watch Uncle Harold unbury you."

Bruce pushed the tray aside and threw back the covers. "I can keep up with you," he said grimly. "Watch." He groped on the floor for his crutches. The drilling, quiet a moment, blasted the morning with a wail that ended as abruptly as it had begun. There was an odd thump, as of earth hitting earth, then a soft hiss of slow shifting gravel that tapered into silence. Carol looked out the window. Her mouth opened, closed soundlessly.

"Bruce."

"What?"

"Parchment Street just fell in the priest tunnel."

X

Bruce balanced himself on his crutches and joined her. He moaned softly. There was a black hole, wide as the street, with workmen standing silent, bewildered at its ragged edges. They looked up vaguely for something in the clear sky that had torn a hole in the earth. Bruce limped to the door and flung it open.

"Dad! Dad!"

Uncle Harold opened the study door, a pen in his hand. He looked up, startled. "What's the matter? What are you doing out of bed?"

"The street fell in—they've ruined the tunnel— they've ruined it—" He set the crutch on the stair beneath him and swung himself down. He sat down abruptly, holding himself. A crutch slid down the stairs, clattering to a rest at Uncle Harold's feet.

"All right," Uncle Harold said hastily. "All right.

175

I'll go and have a look."

He stuck the pen behind his ear and went out the front door. Aunt Catherine came out of the living room.

"What on earth is all the shouting about?"

"The drain fell in the priest tunnel," Carol said. "There's a big hole in Parchment Street."

Aunt Catherine picked up Bruce's crutch. She looked at it a moment, her brows raised thoughtfully. She put it down again suddenly and turned. "I'm going to call Mrs. Brewster."

"What good is that going to do?"

"It may give her someone else to be annoyed with." She went to the kitchen. Bruce sat still, his head in his hands. He raised it abruptly. "I'm going to get dressed. I can't argue with Mrs. Brewster about a priest tunnel in my pajamas."

"Do you think you can get dressed?" Carol said doubtfully. He pulled himself up by the banister.

"I can do anything when I'm desperate enough."

She watched him hop awkwardly up the last steps, clinging to the wall. Then she went outside to look at the hole.

The workmen were arguing with Uncle Harold. They stood around him helplessly, their drills and shovels idle on the pavement.

"What's a tunnel doing under the street? There must be a law against people digging tunnels under public streets where other people might fall into them.

I nearly fell into it—I thought it was an earthquake."

"I doubt if the street was there when it was built," Uncle Harold said. "It's quite old."

"You might have given us a word of warning. Now we'll have all that digging to do over again, not to mention filling the tunnel and paving the road—"

Carol's hands clenched. "You can't fill the tunnel! We worked to open it up, and nobody was paying us, and we didn't even get to go through it because you ruined it."

They stared at her, their faces vague, preoccupied.

"What are we going to do, then? We can't leave it there. You can't expect the Middleton Soccer Team to leap over the hole every time they want to practice. We're being paid to put drains in the street. Nobody's paying us to fix a tunnel that nobody needs."

"They did need it once."

"That was in the old days. Priests don't have to go about in hiding nowadays, so why should they have a tunnel for it? Now they need a road and drains, and that's what we're here for."

Carol stared at them, baffled. She looked at Uncle Harold, who was lighting his pipe. He shook the match out and said reasonably, "After all, it does belong to somebody. It belongs to Mrs. Brewster. She owns the house and everything in it, and this tunnel begins in her cellar."

The workmen looked at each other. "Old Mrs. Brewster?"

177

"Yes."

"Well. Well, it will have to go, anyway. This tunnel is obstructing a public street."

"This street," said Mrs. Brewster, "is obstructing my private tunnel!"

They turned. Uncle Harold, startled, let his pipe die in his hand. She stood neat and proper in the summer morning, a hat with a jeweled buckle on her head, her

white hair gathered without a wisp escaping into a hairnet. Her voice was sound and deep as a church bell. The workmen stood silent with surprise; she continued, her eyes moving sharply across their faces.

"You have thrown your rubble into my priest tunnel. You are obstructing my rights of passage. You have ruined an historical monument in some ridiculous project that is of no use whatsoever except to give me headaches because of the noise, and you have the gall to complain to me about your public streets."

"That rubble down *there* is the public street!"

"May I ask who needs a public street at this particular corner of Middleton? Do you? Or you?" They shifted uneasily, avoiding her eyes.

"What about the Soccer Team bus? It can't drive on the sidewalk!"

Mrs. Brewster drew herself up. She stared at them over the arched bridge of her nose. "Soccer! If a group of grown men whose brains are in their feet cannot manage to walk half a block more to kick a ball about a field, then they have changed very sadly from those men whose courage and faith built this tunnel, and we are in sore straits indeed. What are you laughing about, Harold Lawrence? You have been plaguing me for days about this tunnel; this is no occasion for levity."

Uncle Harold composed himself. "I'm very grateful you've come," he said. "I didn't expect to see you."

Mrs. Brewster sniffed. "I should think not, after what your son did to my flowers."

179

"He didn't do that," Carol said indignantly. "Neither did Alexander. They were opening your priest tunnel when that happened."

Mrs. Brewster's eyes moved to her face. They were black and searching, like birds' eyes, and Carol met them stubbornly.

"In my day," Mrs. Brewster said, "young girls did not run about in bare feet, and they waited until they were introduced before they spoke."

Carol felt her face redden. Her mouth set tightly; her eyes did not move from Mrs. Brewster's face. They gazed at one another across the fallen tunnel.

"I know," she said. "And they didn't have the courage to find out why a girl was walking through a stone wall for three hundred years."

Uncle Harold's hand dropped gently on her shoulder, as if in protection, but Mrs. Brewster was silent. She looked away across the field, her eyes narrowing as though she were trying to see something that had happened a long time before. Then she looked back at Carol, and the rigid lines of her face softened until she was almost smiling.

"I should have guessed. So that is where the tunnel was."

Carol heard Uncle Harold draw a sudden breath. He cleared his throat, as though his voice had not gotten through the first time. "You saw a ghost, too?"

Mrs. Brewster looked around at the ring of silent, staring workmen, and her voice firmed. "You have nearly ruined what should be an historical monument, of more use to the public than this corner of road. I suggest you spend your time now removing that mess of rubble, because that is what you will be ordered to do as soon as I state my grievances to the Middleton Civil Sewage Company."

The workmen looked at each other out of the corners of their eyes. One of them took off his cap and threw it bitterly on the ground. "Priest tunnels. Historical monuments. Why couldn't priests stay in churches where they belong, instead of running about in tunnels—Where does this tunnel end, then?"

Mrs. Brewster looked at Uncle Harold. He shrugged slightly. "Bruce didn't make it to the end."

"And with these imbeciles we may well never know."

"Here!" a workman said indignantly. "There's no need to get personal."

"I," Mrs. Brewster said ominously, "have only just begun."

She turned and went into the yard toward the house. Uncle Harold and Carol followed her. Aunt Catherine was waiting for her at the door.

"Hello, Mrs. Brewster," she said cheerfully. "Have you met my niece, Carol?"

"Yes, I have, Catherine," Mrs. Brewster said. "She is the most sensible person I have met in years. Good morning, Bruce. What are you doing out of bed? You should not inflict the sight of your wan face on healthy people; it's depressing. Where is my tunnel? I wish to go into it."

Bruce blinked. "You can't—I mean, the hole is small, you'll have to sort of wiggle—"

"Then I shall wiggle." She took her hat off carefully and gave it to Aunt Catherine. Bruce looked at Uncle Harold. He was gazing at Mrs. Brewster as though she were something as wondrous and indomitable as the great grey church or the priest tunnel. Bruce turned slowly on his crutches.

"It's in the last room, with all your other antiques."

She went through with Uncle Harold's help. He switched a flashlight on. The light danced across the ancient stones, tracing the curved lines of them. She was silent a moment. She laid one hand lightly on the firm walls.

"I had not expected anything so well-made. Nor did I ever expect to approve anything you instigated, Bruce. You have done well." She turned. "Harold, do you think there are people living who would know how to restore this properly so that one day I can go through it to the end?"

"It's quite possible," Uncle Harold said, helping her back into the cellar. They went upstairs. Mrs. Brewster pinned her hat on.

"I will find such people, as soon as I inform the sewage company that they may not put their drains in my priest tunnel." She paused a moment, looking at Carol. "You questioned my courage. For me, it was not a matter for courage, but a misunderstanding. I only saw the girl once, and living in this house, surrounded by old things, old memories, I simply assumed she was one more rare and beautiful thing that belonged within these old stones. . . . She was a secret and unforgettable dream to me, for I was a passionate, imaginative child. Then I went away to school and I forgot about her. As I grew older, I had less time, less inclination for dreaming. . . . It never occurred to me that she might have had a life, a purpose of her own. How did you guess that I had seen her?"

"You embroidered a picture of her," Carol said softly. "Emily Raison said you copied it from the picture in the study, but you put a wall behind her instead of an arch, because when you saw her, there was a wall behind her."

Mrs. Brewster nodded. "I had forgotten about that. You are quite correct." Her white brows drew together. "That is strange. . . ."

"Yes," Uncle Harold said a little dazedly. "Whoever painted that picture must have known about the tunnel, or guessed it was there, but he was in no position to do more than guess. . . ."

"Yes. I wonder who did it. It was a much more sensible thing to do than to get hysterical as Susan did." The sudden opening of the front door missed her by inches; she turned icily. "I beg your pardon."

"Oh—sorry," Alexander said. Father Malory blushed behind him under Mrs. Brewster's gaze.

"That is no way to open a door."

"It's the only way this one will open. I got somewhat excited when I saw the hole in the street."

"One should never be too excited for common courtesy. Though I admit this is an extraordinary occasion. Good morning, Father Malory. I enjoyed your mass yesterday, although I think it would have sounded less dreadful had you not permitted my grandnephew to sing. It is a pleasure watching young boys do something constructive for a change. If Mrs. Crane writes a letter to the Bishop complaining about you, I shall write to him complaining about Mrs. Crane."

Father Malory's blush deepened. "Thank you. There's no need to write. I have a problem."

"So does the Middleton Civil Sewage Company," Mrs. Brewster said. She turned back to Carol. "Why was the girl going into the priest tunnel?"

"She was leading somebody through. We think he may have been a priest, and she saw him killed or captured by Puritan soldiers. There were other ghosts; they were waiting for him in the tunnel."

"Good heavens," Mrs. Brewster said. "And you and Bruce had the patience to unravel such a mystery? Why did you not get hysterical and run?"

"Where?" Bruce said. "I live here."

Mrs. Brewster looked at him, almost surprised. Then she said dryly, "There are many ways of running. I imagine you know most of them. I am grateful to you both, and to you, Alexander. When the tunnel is made safe, you will be the first to see where it ends."

Father Malory gave a soft cough behind her. "It ends in the church broom closet."

They stared at him. Uncle Harold said weakly, "How on earth do you know?"

"I told you I have a problem. I followed the ghost yesterday—"

"You followed the ghost!"

"I lied to you. It wasn't actually a lie, but I intended it to be. I misled you—"

"Stop quibbling," Mrs. Brewster said. "And stop interrupting, Harold."

"I didn't go to see Mrs. Murphy. I went down and waited in the cellar until four o'clock. You see, there was no one else to do it, and I knew how disappointed Bruce and Carol would be if it were walled up before they could know where it ended. I didn't see the ghosts, but I trusted that they had seen them. So at four o'clock I went through to the end." He paused. "You were quite right to stay out. The mortar seems to be cracking in quite a few places. Well. I found Edward. That's my problem. I'm not sure what to do with a three-hundred-year-old set of bones."

The hall was silent. Bruce lowered himself onto the bottom stair.

"I knew it," Carol said tightly. "I knew they killed him in front of her."

"Are you sure it was Edward?" Uncle Harold asked.

"There were bits of black cloth on the bones . . .

I think they must have closed the tunnel then, with the same stones that they had used to build the wall. That's why there was no trace of it." He paused again. A gentle morning wind set the leaves chattering above the wall. "There was a silver cross on a chain that had fallen between the ribs. . . . I suspect he was a priest. Perhaps that's what kept her—awake. The feeling that he was dead, walled in the tunnel, with no one to know, no one to mourn him, as well as her anger against the men who had killed him and gone unpunished."

"That poor child," Aunt Catherine said wonderingly. "Why don't you bury him?"

"I thought of that. But I'm not sure. . . . He's probably an Anglican priest. I could give his bones to Father Nichols of St. Martin's parish, but that would involve a bit of explaining, and Father Nichols is an admirable man, but eminently—factual."

"On the other hand," Uncle Harold said, "if he had been buried, he probably would have been buried across the street, since his family was here."

Father Malory nodded. "It's only that I don't want to bury him in the wrong place and have the girl wandering about unhappy. She's very persistent."

"I don't think she'd care where he was buried," Carol said, "as long as she knew somebody else cared that he was buried."

"I hardly think he would have spent this much time himself arguing about where his bones were to be laid," Mrs. Brewster said tartly. Father Malory turned to her.

"I disagree," he said mildly. "People's feelings about religion were very intense and very intolerant then. If a man died for a particular faith, he wouldn't want to be buried in somebody else's graveyard. The girl may feel just as intensely."

"I should think," Aunt Catherine said, "that after three hundred years, she may feel like taking a rest."

"Perhaps you're right. I'll put him in our graveyard then; after all these centuries there should be a good mixture of Catholic and Anglican bones. But I'm not sure what to do with that animal."

"What animal?"

He shook his head. "I'm not sure what it is. A small dog, perhaps, or a cat. It's lying beside him. It was apparently trapped when the tunnel was closed."

Carol made a small, inarticulate sound. She dropped beside Bruce and said breathlessly, "That cat! The black cat—You saw him, Uncle Harold." The laughter welled in her, sudden and senseless, and she yielded to it, leaning against the banisters, giggling weakly. "It kept disappearing in the cellar—It was a ghost." She heard Bruce whimper beside her; he gasped. "Please— Don't make me laugh—it hurts—"

"I can't help it; it's so funny. Uncle Harold always thought it was real, and all the time it was three hundred years old, running around looking for its bones—"

"I yield," Uncle Harold said. His voice quivered

helplessly. "The evidence is overwhelming."

Mrs. Brewster gazed down at their tearful faces. "Really," she said. "Bruce Lawrence, if you could have laughed like that six months ago you would not have felt like being such a source of intolerable annoyance to your neighbors."

They went down to the cellar at a quarter to four and sat among Mrs. Brewster's antiques on her table. Specks of mortar dust revolved in the sunlight from the broken window. Bruce traced a pattern in the pale dust on the floor with the end of his crutch.

"Dad says we'll go to Scotland as soon as I can walk decently. So you'll have a whole week there, at least. You'll like camping."

"Then I'll have to go back home. And then back to school. . . ." She sighed. "Nothing exciting ever happens at school. Nothing this exciting will ever happen again."

"You don't have to worry about that now. Worry some other time."

The cellar door opened and closed. They were quiet, listening to the soft footsteps on the stairs. Alexander came through the rooms toward them. He smiled.

"I thought you might be here. If she comes, I'll cry. You've never seen me cry, have you? I can do it as well as Roger Simmons." He sat down on a book box.

"If she comes," Bruce said, "I'm giving up."

"She won't come," Carol said. "I bet she won't. Edward's bones aren't in there anymore. There's nothing to come back for."

"I hope you're right. I'm so tired of thinking about her that a corner of my brain is all worn out."

"Properly speaking," Alexander said, "a brain doesn't have corners. It's all rounded, with grooves, and what she's done is worn a groove in your mind, so you'll never forget her."

"That's all I need. A groove with a ghost in it." He looked at Carol. "Are you ever going to tell anyone about her and Edward?"

"I was thinking about that," Carol said slowly. She picked up a tiny china golden-haired shepherdess and frowned at it absently, tracing the lines of it with her fingers. "My friends will ask me 'What is England like?' and they'll be thinking of castles and those guards with the big fur hats, and rock groups. And I'll be thinking of a cellar underneath an old house with a tunnel and a ghost in it. Things are different from the way you think they'll be. I don't know. Maybe I will, except my mother would worry. She wouldn't believe me, because she can't see the tunnel, and she would think I was coming down with something. I could tell my best friend. But I don't think she even believes in history. It's hard to, when all the houses and stores and freeways and buildings around you are so new. But I suppose I will tell, because it's so exciting that it would be too hard not to talk about, but . . . I don't really think anyone will believe me. Not really. I wouldn't believe me."

"Will that matter to you?" Alexander asked softly. She shook her head, smiling.

"No."

The bells played their slow, familiar melody into the still afternoon. They rang four steady, strong notes, casually as though there were not three people listening to them without moving, without breathing, still as the antique figurines on the dusty table. The faint echo of bells seemed to linger unendurably in the silence. Bruce's shoulders lowered. He drew a long breath. He caught Carol's smile and laughed suddenly.

"Say it. Say I told you so. Have the last word."

"I told you so," she said contentedly.